MUTINY AT THE MANOR

Tapestry Tales
Book Two

Cara Clayton

SAPERE
BOOKS

MUTINY AT
THE MANOR

Published by Sapere Books.

24 Trafalgar Road, Ilkley, LS29 8HH

saperebooks.com

ISBN: 978-0-85495-778-1

PROLOGUE

Lincolnshire, 1380

Clémence Amundeville lay back on the pillows. Her granddaughter, Elizabeth, took the frail fingers in her own and watched the gentle smile appear on the cherished face of her grandmother. She stroked the whisps of hair away from the old lady's forehead and remembered the precious times she had shared with this amazing lady. Sitting on her knee before the embroidery panels that told the story of their lives past and present; standing on a stool as she stirred the mix for the Christmas plum pudding as they thickened it with breadcrumbs; running through the orchard and sinking among the petals that drifted like snowflakes as they giggled together; lying in her bed under the heavy covers and being told tales of times past as Clémence soothed her to sleep. Always Clémence, rarely her own mother.

Now, she was old enough to understand Mary's frailties and knew it was her task, and that of her fourteen-year-old brother Rogier, to protect their parent. Their father had been killed at the Battle of Pontvallain in the Sarthe region of north-west France ten years earlier. The English had suffered heavily when the French army under Bertrand de Guesclin had defeated an English force that had broken away from the main army commanded by Sir Robert Knolles. But as a child she had barely known her father and when he didn't return, she hadn't missed him. Her days were content with Rogier and her adored grandparents.

Elizabeth pushed her chestnut locks away from her face as she leaned in to hear Clémence's soft voice. "You have been my joy, my treasure. You've become a beautiful young lady and you are honourable, if sometimes too adventurous," she added with a twinkle in her eye. "Be proud, my sweeting. I know you and Rogier will take care of your mother, but look to your own self too. You will seek happiness and contentment for others and in so doing you will find your own, dearest child. Here, keep this in memory of me, dear one. I hope you find as great a love as I have been blessed."

She pressed a small, gold annular brooch into Elizabeth's palm. It was engraved with the names of both her grandparents, which had been given and received with deepest love on their wedding day. She glanced across at her grandfather, Ruadhán, sitting next to them, his head bowed, lips moving in silent prayer.

Clémence exhaled as her eyes slowly closed as she slipped away from them silently. Her fingers slackened as Ruadhán's own tightened around her hand. Elizabeth's arm slid around Ruadhán's shoulders as tears seeped from his eyes with grief.

CHAPTER 1

Elizabeth cleansed the body of her grandmother with wine and sweet herbs to ensure any sins were wiped away. Clémence had the best of souls while alive. Surely her visit to Purgatory would be minimal before moving on towards blessed rest in the arms of the Lord. Later, goodwives would wrap Clémence in clean linen, and the casket in which she would be placed would rest under the lych gate of Edenham church, guarded by the most trusted sokemen until her brother arrived to take on that responsibility. Since she was not noble-born, unlike her husband, there would be no ceremony at the Folkingham castle chapel but, finally, following a service inside the church she would be laid to rest under a stone near the altar, for she had been married to a noble knight.

As dawn broke, painting the sky with soft hues of peach and pale grey, Elizabeth stretched her back, looked to the open window embrasure, and breathed in the freshness of the grass as it soaked up the dew of the night.

Typically, her thoughts turned to practical issues. She must send word to her brother. Rogier had been called to the castle at Folkingham, a few leagues from their manor at Grimsthorpe in Lincolnshire. He had to continue his duties as a squire before knighthood. Little stopped for the necessities of war and this one with France dragged on with battle after battle. It had already lasted almost fifty years — with intermittent ferocity over territorial rights and issues of succession to the French throne — and still there was no end in sight. In fact, the conflict had grown broader to involve factions across

Western Europe, with each new monarch fuelled by emerging nationalism on all sides.

Having left her grandfather to his prayers with Father Bernard, Elizabeth sought out the copper-lidded box she had recently discovered when clearing her grandmother's room. The wooden box with its ornate hinges was filled with treasured personal items Clémence had collected throughout her life. Her own mother must have hidden it away and added nothing. Elizabeth determined that she would continue the tradition, beginning with her inclusion of the small gold brooch her grandmother had given her as she breathed her last.

She would look forwards again and start a new panel for the embroidered tapestry that told the tales of their lives and maybe, in the future, some other young lady would find her additions in the copper treasure box.

Elizabeth decided to leave the manor house for a short walk. She needed to retreat for an hour from all the problems beginning to mount. Her grandfather was still grieving the loss of his beloved wife despite the passing of several weeks and, as a result, many of the jobs that needed doing around the manor had been neglected. The most pressing was the need to appoint a new bailiff, the last having passed away some weeks ago. Marcus Smith was a satisfactory reeve but all the decisions awaiting a bailiff were beyond him. The steward was busy with household affairs, Mary was constantly vacillating, and Elizabeth was loathe to pester her grandfather, but the lack of decision-making regarding the livestock, the rotation of crops, and the buying and selling of goods was starting to show. Decisions about which animals to keep and which to sell were needed. Stocks of salt, parchment, nails, and iron would be out of kilter and their own piles of skins and wood were starting to mount and should be sold. If Rogier were home from Folkingham she would consult him, young as he was, but in his absence Elizabeth simply had to do her best to oversee the smooth running of the manor.

She crossed the wooden bridge over the moat, towards the woods. The bells at the monastery had rung terce some time ago and the sun was rising higher, although there was time before she must return for the midday meal. The day was clear and the warmth of the sun welcome. She looked up and gloried in the cloudless blue sky. A lark ascending from the fields was also enjoying the freshness of the morning and gave a full-throated burst of joyful merriment.

"Good morning," Elizabeth called as she passed the first cottage. A child was teasing wool and removing the noyles, the short broken fibres and impurities, as she repeatedly pulled the carding combs across it. A woman was sitting beside her on a stump of wood spinning — that never-ending task of village life. If it wasn't weaving wool into cloth suitable for clothing, it was linen for the swaddling of the next infant to be born. Thirty years had passed since the pestilence had decimated their community. The population was slowly increasing once more, but there was still a shortage of labour, with fewer men to farm the land or women to support them. Even here, at Grimsthorpe and Folkingham, despite the lengths to which Clémence and Ruadhán had gone to protect their workers, the losses had been great.

The woman nodded at Elizabeth before standing and bobbing a curtsey.

"There's no need," Elizabeth said, giving her a warm smile and waving her back down. "It's not so many years since my family lived in a cottage similar to yours." She knew her family had a greater standing than many; her great-grandfather having been a free master mason at King John's Tower and the monastery. Yet it was her grandmother, Clémence, who had risen above this status to become lady of the manor. Elizabeth had only to glance down at her fine linen and silk clothing and the woven wool worn by the villager to see how the sumptuary laws strengthened the social hierarchy.

As she walked on she met a man on the path. A mattock rested over his shoulder. "Good day, Master Pullen. I see you are on your way to remove the thistles." She nodded at the tool. "I hope the crops are growing well for you?"

He grunted but didn't touch his forelock as she expected. She didn't seek that mark of respect, but she was surprised that he hadn't acknowledged her status as a daughter of the manor.

"Ah, mistress, there's much to do and I am still to find time to dig the field drainage over yonder that Master Reeve demanded." He tossed his head in the direction of the lower field that tended to flood during inclement weather. "It was hard enough before the pestilence took half our people."

"When we have a new bailiff, perhaps he may attract more vassals to our land and you will have less to do." Elizabeth understood this was not easy. The surrounding estates were in the same position and recently it had been decreed that movement of villeins from one holding to another was not allowed.

"Huh! Chance will be a fine thing." Master Pullen shrugged and moved off.

At that moment, a small group of estate workers approached, each carrying the tools of their work on the land. At this time of year it was mattocks for cutting, adzes for grubbing the hard soil, pitchforks for scooping the rubbish and depositing it in piles, and spades for clearing the stubborn roots. Their voices were loud and they appeared to be arguing. On seeing Elizabeth, they unshouldered their implements and pointed them towards her. If she hadn't known each of them better, she might have felt threatened. As it was, she hesitated and surveyed their angry expressions with wariness.

"Ah, Mistress Elizabeth," said one. "We were just talking of you an' those up at the manor." He looked her straight in the eyes while others within the group scuffed the ground with the toes of their boots.

"Good day to you," Elizabeth said, glancing around at the assembled company. "At least it's a fine day with a mild spring sun for your labours."

"That's as may be," said the man, "but there's still more work than we can do with those of us who are left."

"That's just what I was saying," said Master Pullen, joining the company.

"We need some leeway on what we can do."

"Or more wages for the work we are doing," another man mumbled.

"Things are still really hard," Elizabeth explained. "We're not growing and gathering as much, so we don't have as much surplus to sell. We have the land but not enough people to tend it, yet we still need to buy. Many of our trading networks have disintegrated. Things are…" She stopped short of saying things were a mess. There was little point in stating the obvious and giving the men greater cause for anxiety and displeasure.

There was muttering among the men. Elizabeth was at a loss to know what to say. Then the spokesman for the group said, "It's all well for his lordship, but we haven't seen him for weeks now. What are we supposed to do? We can't keep going like this and Master Reeve doesn't help. There's no talking to him. He won't listen."

Elizabeth stepped back, shocked at the effrontery.

Some dared to nod at the outrageous words about their lord and master, though it was true that Sir Ruadhán had not left his solar for many days.

Suddenly there was a cloud of dust in the distance and the unmistakable sound of hooves on the hardened earth. Elizabeth looked around the men to see who might be approaching, which caused them to turn also.

A cart approached and Elizabeth was relieved to see the horse was driven by Gabriel Smith, younger brother to the reeve, Marcus, who sat beside him. As they came level with the small crowd of workers, they saluted her presence.

"Your ladyship," said Marcus. Then he turned to the men. What's going on here?"

"We were having a discussion," Elizabeth proclaimed before any of the men could reply, for she understood they could be in trouble with Marcus should they continue in the same vein with him.

"Best get to your work," Marcus said. "Haven't you enough to do? I can easily find work for idle hands."

With heads down and in silent belligerence, the group of men drifted away.

"Mistress, will you take a ride home with us?" Gabriel jumped down from the running board. He offered Elizabeth his hand to help her climb up the spokes of the wheel to sit between them.

"Thank you," she said, trying to ignore her confusion as his bright azure eyes sent shivers through her. "It's been a while since we spoke."

"Aye. 'Tis many a year since we ran as children among the stooks of the harvest or played tag among the trees."

"Indeed, it is. Many summers have passed since then and…" She was going to remark on the different trajectories their lives had taken but deemed it inappropriate since she was at the manor house and he lived in a house in the village.

She turned to include Marcus in the conversation. "Are you well, sir?"

"What was all that about?" Marcus asked, ignoring her pleasantry. "Not more grumbling about their workload, I hope?"

"They want more land of their own, or higher wages, Brother," Gabriel said before Elizabeth could reply.

"More land? They hardly do what's necessary now."

"That may be, but if the land was their own with the possibility of greater yields from which they would benefit directly, they would work harder, I'm sure."

"That's not going to happen. The demesne is making less now than it did ten years ago, and the workforce is too small to farm it all now that the population is only half what it was before the Great Mortality."

Elizabeth could see the conundrum, but Marcus seemed unable to grasp his brother's point of view. She was interested in Gabriel's ideas but said nothing more. What she did know, however, was that something had to be done. However, she was in a quandary for it should be her grandfather or even her mother who should act.

CHAPTER 2

Elizabeth missed her younger brother. They had always been close and she relied on discussing things with him. While the position of lord of the manor was still filled by her grandfather, she was loathe to bother him, but she could see that Ruadhán was ailing, sinking further into a miasma of sorrow despite there being a thousand things that needed to be done. It was a major frustration to Elizabeth that her mother dithered over every small thing and was incapable of making decisions with the steward about the household, never mind the reeve with regard to land management. Clémence's determination and common sense had certainly missed a generation, and since Elizabeth's father had been slaughtered in north-west France, Mary had not coped at all. It was no wonder dissension was beginning to bubble among the workers. If Rogier were here she could at least seek his opinion, though she suspected he was much more interested in enjoying his time at the castle on the tiltyard or riding out with the other squires and knights, hunting, or talking with soldiers garrisoned at King John's Tower.

It was with relief that, only days later, she heard the sound of hooves and the pounding of feet on the bridge over the moat and by the time she reached the great oak door, her brother and his entourage of friends and menservants were dismounting in the courtyard and calling for the groomsmen. With Rogier's arrival there was immediate action. Men ran to do his bidding and deep voices echoed off the stone walls. Elizabeth hurried to find Mary and tell the household staff to prepare extra courses for dinner. After giving her brother a merry hug, she waited until the young men were standing around the fireplace quaffing mugs of ale before dashing up the stairs to Ruadhán's solar to impart the news.

"Grandfather," she said, "Rogier has returned from Folkingham Castle. Would you like to come down and hear his news. Sir John, Lord de Beaumont, has recently returned from court and Rogier will have heard what has been happening in London with King Richard." Elizabeth regarded her grandfather. The old man was in his chair, shrouded by a blanket despite the mildness of the day. He looked thin and frail, his cheeks sunken and dark shadows beneath his eyes.

He looked up at her with a fleeting flare of engagement, before it faded. "Tell him to come to me when he is rested and dined. There is no hurry for I may sleep for a while."

Elizabeth bent to kiss his forehead, breathing in the dear scent of him. He gave her a gentle smile and raised his remaining arm to touch her cheek, and her heart fluttered for the shadow of the man he was before Clémence died. She remembered the warmth of those fingers as they steadied her as she learned to ride, to shoot an arrow, to hunt with her peregrine falcon. He had laughed and teased when she determined to master the flight and landing of the larger, heavier gyrfalcon.

As she returned to the hall, talk had turned to the national and international problems of the day. King Richard was only thirteen and had been thrust into the position of ruler following the death of his father Edward, Prince of Wales from a severe recurrence of the flux three years previously.

"The king's uncles, John of Gaunt and Thomas of Woodstock, may not have been given the regency but they still hold much influence over the business of government," Rogier said.

"They and the other councillors are becoming increasingly unpopular, apparently," another noble said.

"Have a care with what you say," Rogier said.

"I do but speak the truth. And what about this poll tax? Even Gaunt's own son, Henry of Bolingbroke, raised noises against it, and he's nearly a neighbour here in Lincolnshire."

John of Gaunt held vast lands and huge connections. Bolingbroke castle and the surrounding estates, where Henry was born, was the major administrative centre for the Duchy of Lancaster. John was granted the county of Lincolnshire upon his first marriage to Blanche. Thus he was overlord for Folkingham castle and the Beaumonts and the will of the richest and most powerful man in the land must not be gainsaid.

"The war with France must be funded somehow," said Rogier.

Another, Sir Alaric Swain, spoke up. "It might be easier to accept the extra taxes if the war was going well. Those early victories have not been repeated. Gaunt may have done well at the Battle of Nájera but it was hardly repeated during the St Malmo affair. He couldn't even raise enough ships to transport the horses and troops, and when he thought the war with France was unwinnable, the Truce of Bruges didn't last. At least old King Edward and the Prince of Wales saw victory in battle."

"I want to get over there," Rogier declared. "My grandfather was a hero. I'd love to share that glory."

"Perhaps there are battles to win closer to home," said Sir Alaric. "Our labourers aren't happy. These rumblings of unrest need to be quashed."

"One groat for every person over the age of fourteen is a high price to pay," said another.

"Four pence, yes, especially when it's across all and takes no account of ability to pay. Lord John at Folkingham said it raised twenty-two thousand pounds in that first year." Sir Alaric quaffed deeply from his cup.

"But maintaining our presence in Calais and Brest alone cost thirty-six thousand, I heard him say," Elizabeth muttered.

All eyes turned to her, some with surprise that a young lady would know such information, while others frowned at her intrusion.

She shrugged and added, "When the Crown returned for more money last year, it only raised eighteen and a half thousand when fifty thousand was required. There is much evasion of payment. Perhaps a different strategy is needed."

"Mistress Elizabeth is correct, and with the war going so badly now, Sir Simon of Sudbury said one hundred and sixty thousand would be needed. You would think the Lord Chancellor would have done the sums correctly," said Sir Alaric, looking with an appraising eye upon Elizabeth and seeming to like what he saw, judging by the smile that played across his face. He continued, "We may need to be on our mettle at home if the noises I have been hearing about the workers is true, although I doubt they would be so foolish as to argue with their masters and betters." He manoeuvred his way to stand next to Elizabeth. "Do not fear, Mistress Elizabeth, there are several of us here to protect you should any trouble erupt."

She lowered her eyes but inside she bristled. *I can take care of myself and my people*, she thought.

"The order of things has been as it is for centuries. Surely our Lord John of Gaunt and Duke of Lancaster knows wisely what he does at court," one young knight said.

"So, Mistress Elizabeth," Sir Alaric continued, "we look forward to eating at your table this evening, and perhaps you will regale us with more of your informed opinion." Alaric looked around at his friends for approval and when they smirked with him, she gave him a frosty look. His charming manner and good looks made her blush, but he clearly had enough arrogance to know it and Elizabeth determined to maintain her distance.

The dinner the kitchens had managed to put together was indeed a feast. The pottage, enriched with balls of skinless sausage meat, was followed by a pudding of cowcumber. The finely chopped pork, raisins, and crumbs held together with eggs and flavoured with mace, pepper and cloves sat in the scooped vegetables.

As the capon pie was served, Elizabeth heard her brother speak. "Baron John said the latest at court is that our Lord of Gaunt wants to replace the elected mayor of London with a court appointment. I tell you, there is considerable unrest at the top."

"But Sir William Walworth is the representative of the aldermen, he cannot be sacked."

"Exactly! It's making the Duke of Lancaster most unpopular, especially with the other measures he is pushing."

"Our lord wishes for a change because Mayor Walworth suppressed usury in the city. Have a care, Rogier, our Lord at Folkingham, as a liegeman to the duke, will not be happy if you imply our Lord of Gaunt is at fault," Sir Alaric said. "You can't blame the duke for manoeuvring to enrich himself where he can, and he can afford to lend money with ease. His lands and the people on them benefit in the end. What say you, Mistress Elizabeth?"

Sir Alaric caught her eye and winked. Her cheeks must have flushed which caused him amusement. He was undeniably attractive but she refused to be drawn; instead she demurred and said she knew little of such things. In truth her opinions and allegiances were clear. Her people were suffering and the instability between the ruling classes at court were not helping them. Perhaps Mayor Walworth was correct to limit the rich from making more money by charging an exorbitant rate when lending it.

"I'm only suggesting that usury is unethical if it makes money for the lender through immoral loans with outrageous interest rates. I'm not saying that's what our Lord Gaunt has done, though. I know Baron John is the duke's man and therefore so are we." Rogier waved his cup as he lounged in his chair, and Elizabeth could tell he was well-surfeited with mead and becoming careless. She turned in her seat and clapped her hands to call for the soft stewed pears, rysschews of fruits and pottage of ris flavoured with almonds to be served.

Relief flooded Elizabeth when the conversation turned from politics to a hunting escapade in which a good-sized boar and two stags were downed. She was happy to watch the young men as conversation flowed. Sir Alaric was interesting, indeed, and she found her eyes wandering to him with frequency, but she was unsure of the wisdom of some of his pronouncements.

The Lenten lilies and bluebells had all finished flowering when Ruadhán finally joined his beloved wife. Through all the trials of war and plague Clémence had been at his side to support him, taking the lead at times, and together they had built a happy and fruitful demesne. Without her strength and love he had been unable to continue, rarely leaving his solar, eating little and showing no interest in manor life, until he simply faded away.

Elizabeth retrieved her grandmother's treasure box and ran her fingers over the tiny stone inserts placed in the wood that decorated the lid. It was ageing and one was loose. It must not be lost from this valuable heirloom. She would have to ask one of the men to secure it with wax or pitch. She lifted the hasp that secured the lid. The items inside told the story of Clémence and Ruadhán's life together, for they were together, absolutely, even when he had been away fighting for his king for extended periods of time. The embroidered tapestry told the story of their lives. Tiny wooden figurines, birds and animals whittled by Ruadhán, were dated on the underside — small gifts punctuating their time together. There was a peacock's tail feather wrapped in fine silk. It came from one of the first birds to be introduced to the country by Sir John de Foxley — Ruadhán had purchased a pair of birds from him for Clémence's entertainment. She believed, as did others, that the 'eye' on the tail feathers brought them harmony and peace throughout their married life. No wonder she had cared for it. The progeny of this pair of birds still wandered the orchard and gardens. Elizabeth replaced the iridescent feather in its silk wrapping with care.

Lastly, she took out the gold annular brooch so recently placed in the treasure box. Perhaps she should wear it rather than hide it away. It had been one of Clémence's favourites and she remembered her grandmother wearing it many times. She fingered the tiny engraving of her grandparents' names and the small sword-shaped pin that held it to the wearer's clothes. Its intrinsic value to her was greater than it's worth to others and although the most recent updated sumptuary laws prevented the servants from owning such a piece, she wouldn't want to put temptation in anyone's way, so she placed it back in the box.

The family had prepared Sir Ruadhán Amundeville's body with care, sat vigil and said prayers over the last few days in the hope that his soul would have a short passage through Purgatory before finding peace in the Kingdom of Heaven. He lay within his casket, his body having been cleansed with good white wine and rubbed with herbs and spices so that any sins — though few they must be — were washed away, before being placed to rest in full armour. Elizabeth had gathered flowers and placed them with her dear grandfather before those that had gathered passed before him, said their prayers for his soul, and the casket was sealed.

The service was held in the church of Folkingham Castle. The landed gentry were present, including Sir John, 4th Lord Beaumont, despite his important duties to the king as Privy Councillor, Admiral of the North, Constable of Dover Castle, Warden of the Cinque Ports, and Ambassador to France. His new wife, Lady Katherine Beaumont, accompanied him and the Amundeville family were honoured by his rare presence, so frequently was he away on court business.

The coffin had crossed the outer and then the inner moat of the castle, entering the rectangular site by way of the bridge on the west side. In procession, Mary, accompanied by Elizabeth and Rogier, were followed by the younger knights and squires of Rogier's acquaintance. Many of the estate workers had been granted leave to follow the family as far as the inner moat and there, were pleased to seat themselves on the grass to rest and wait with silent respect.

This was the passing and laying to rest of one the important and well-respected knights of the region who had fought for his king and protected them through the most terrible times of the Great Pestilence. All current unrest and grievances were laid aside for the time being.

The service was long and as Elizabeth sat in the church her mind wandered. She understood most of the Latin, unlike many. Her grandmother had taught her much, as she herself had learned from the monks at Vaudey Abbey as a girl. Her gaze wandered over the congregation.

The higher ranking sokemen were granted the rights of their station and stood towards the back of the nave or in the side aisles, while Sir John's family and the Amundevilles sat on either side of the crossing so they could see the quire, the pulpit, the shrines, and the sanctuary in front of the altar. The Father Prior from Vaudey was a small, rotund man and took his place at the ambo to read the psalms.

Elizabeth's mind continued its ramblings. It had been a relief when Ruadhán had bequeathed the manor and all its lands to herself and Rogier, rather than his daughter Mary, who was ill-equipped to manage on her own. They must appoint a new bailiff soon. It was critical for the smooth running of the demesne. Her attention was caught by Gabriel Smith's countenance — he stood half a head taller than most. Was he watching her with his azure eyes? The curl of a smile suggested he was. His brother, Marcus, stood next to him, but while he had the same dark good looks, his countenance was surly. She looked away with haste.

On the other side of the crossing sat the young noblemen of the Beaumont household. They all looked dashing in their close-fitting hose and jerkins of their lord's bright *azure semée* livery. Sir John's attire was fully covered in the fleur-de-lis motifs adopted by the previous king in his bid to claim the French throne, and the lion rampant clearly denoted his allegiance. Each young knight had fashionable chaperon headgear although one or two favoured the smaller hats with folded brim. As her eyes roved the faces of those seated she saw Sir Alaric. He was watching her and she had to scold herself for her beating heart and return her concentration to the priest.

Following the conclusion of the service the family made their way back to Edenham as Ruadhán had requested, where they held the emotional committal. After they said their final goodbyes to Ruadhán as he joined Clémence in the family vault, there was a general milling about outside as people paid their respects to Mary. Elizabeth stood by her side while Rogier spoke with acquaintances and neighbours who had come to say their farewells to the knight of known bravery and dedication. As the family prepared to take their leave and return to the manor at Grimsthorpe, a tall man with a slight paunch approached.

"My dear lady," he bent his head over Mary's hand, the breeze blowing his wispy hair around his neck. His lips did not quite touch her hand and his head was only slightly inclined, demonstrating that he saw himself as her equal. "You may not remember me. Sir Bartholomew de'Ath at your service. My condolences on your loss. And now you are alone in this world with a sizeable demesne to run. It must be a worry for you."

"She is not quite alone, sir," said Elizabeth. There was something about this fawning man she did not like. "My brother, Sir Rogier, and I are on hand to give what support our mother may require."

"Of course," he said.

"And we have an excellent reeve, and are soon to appoint a bailiff. My grandfather's appointees within the house are fully trustworthy, so all is in hand."

Sir Bartholomew ignored her and looked back to Mary. "You may remember that I own a substantial and profitable wool business with first-class flocks of sheep. If I can be of any assistance at all please send a messenger immediately. God go with you, my dear. And with your youngsters," he added, turning briefly to Elizabeth and Rogier.

A chill breeze swept the graveyard. "Come, Mother," Elizabeth took Mary's arm, "let us return home."

CHAPTER 3

"Reading and writing are important skills for the bailiff," said Mary.

Elizabeth smiled. "Indeed." She was relieved that her mother had at last agreed to discuss the appointment of a bailiff for the manor. Her enthusiasm was short-lived as Mary shook her head.

"Oh, it's all so difficult. Why did my father leave me like this? He should be here to take charge of things."

"Rogier and I are here to help you, Mother."

"Yes, but Rogier isn't old enough and anyway, he's hardly here, always away training or at King John's Tower with the garrison or at the castle in Folkingham." She threw a shifty look at her son, who pursed his lips in displeasure.

"He must go where Lord John dictates," Elizabeth responded quickly. "We are fortunate that he is not away at war, and that Lord John is working in London with the Privy Council rather than fighting in France." She turned the conversation back to the matter at hand. "The new bailiff must know all about sowing, harvesting and threshing. Then there's the ploughing and when to shear the sheep. Oh, and he must know about the buying and selling of the wood and our animal pelts. Our stocks are building and we need to release the money from them if we are to remain profitable."

"It's too complicated. Perhaps I should consult the gentleman who offered his help at Father's laying to rest. He seems to know about such things. Oh what was his name? De Ath, that was it."

"Mother, I may not have yet reached my majority," said Rogier, "but Grandfather gave Elizabeth and I his permission to run the demesne. He was clear about that and it is written. I think between us we are able to make this decision without that man's advice."

Elizabeth seized the moment. "Absolutely. We know the people on our own property far better than anyone else. I'm certain we may make a sensible choice."

"My cousin's boy is of an age and not living far away," murmured Mary distractedly. "Perhaps we might send a messenger and he might take on the role of bailiff?"

Elizabeth sighed. "Mother, you must know it's not recommended to have a close friend or relative in such a role. It would risk accusations against the family when he is given accommodation in the manor as well as his monthly money. The bailiff must collect rents, which can make him unpopular with the tenants, so it's best if he is not related directly to us. There is already unrest among the workers — we don't need any more."

"Then perhaps we could ask Goodman Steward who he thinks may be suitable. He has worked on our estate for many years."

"We know our people as well as the steward, if not better," said Rogier. "I shall decide. Elizabeth and I shall discuss it further when next I am here." He placed his hand on Mary's arm and endeavoured to soothe her anxiety. "In the meantime calm yourself, all will be well."

"Yes, yes," she mumbled. "I think I shall go to my solar and decide what I might wear to market next week. I must wear black for several more months, but I think it would be permissible to change from my white linen headdress to black, now we are in the second stage of the mourning period.

Perhaps I might add a dark blue ribbon. That would be acceptable, would it not?"

"It would, Mother," replied Elizabeth with a weak smile.

"It's not too soon, is it?" Mary suddenly looked worried. "I shouldn't want to risk my soul by moving on too quickly, but then it is my father, and not my husband, who has moved on into the afterlife."

Elizabeth realised the thorny problem of the appointment of the bailiff had passed Mary by. She would discuss it with Rogier upon his return the following week. Surely the issue would be solved then, for the huge piles of pelts and wood were mounting with each day.

Rogier had enjoyed being a page to Sir John, Lord Beaumont, but as a squire his training had moved on. He understood that even mundane tasks like cleaning weapons and polishing armour were meaningful and he took pride in doing those things. His book learning — reading, writing, Latin and French — with Lady Katherine and the monks from Vaudey Abbey were also important, but they were nothing compared to the excitement of horsemanship, dressing for battle, and demonstrating his skills in the tilt yard. As for hunting, falconry and the banter among the other squires that accompanied these activities, there was nothing to rival it. He was determined to become a knight and worked hard in every practical area, aware that his progress was being watched with interest.

He had attended the knighting ceremony of Alaric Swain a few months previously. Prior to the formal dubbing, Alaric had washed and shaved before spending the night in the church, his sword raised above him on the altar where he reflected upon the honours and perils that awaited him. When he had arrived for the ceremony two knights had dressed him in white with a similar coloured belt to symbolise his purity. Brown tights representing the earth to which he would eventually return and a red cloak to show his awareness of the blood he would be prepared to shed completed his ensemble.

All this awaited Rogier. The final glory was the presentation of gilded spurs and the double-edged sword, one representing justice and the other loyalty and chivalry. Such was Rogier's destiny and he could not wait.

The following week the weather was warm, the sun shone and birds were singing joyously. A walk up to King John's Tower and its practice yard beckoned Elizabeth. It was good to be outside after a week of work and completing daily mundane tasks around the manor.

As she approached the tower she looked up at the thick, crenelated walls with their arrow slits. The sun shone on the large grey stones with its orange lichen, bringing a warmth to the fortification. The thundering of hooves as the men practised their skills rumbled up from the ground and made Elizabeth's neck tingle. She never tired of watching the strength of the knights and squires as they wielded their lances, riding at the rings or the quintain. The cheers that arose from those watching when a lance scooped the small rings from the hook, or the jeers when a man missed the quintain and it continued its circular swing, nearly knocking him off his horse, was highly entertaining. On the far side of the arena some soldiers from the regular garrison were stripped to the waist, slick with sweat, wrestling and lifting heavy weights. Elizabeth spotted Sir Alaric among the group.

A voice behind her made her jump.

"My lady." Gabriel stood at her shoulder. "It's a fine sight, is it not," he said with a cheeky grin. "Mind you, it's a serious business, training to kill. Still, it saves you and I having to train like that," he said, before murmuring, "although I would defend our manor estates."

Elizabeth was surprised by the weight of his comment. She asked, "Are you here for the purpose of work on this beautiful day, Master Smith?" She instantly regretted sounding superior in her position as lady of the manor.

Gabriel appeared to take no umbrage. "I had a delivery to make to the garrison at the tower but I shall be on my way. Enjoy your view." He grinned as he walked away.

Elizabeth watched him leave. His stride was confident and his back straight, ensuring poise and presence. His dark hair curled about his head, but it was his blue eyes that were particularly arresting. One minute they were glinting with mischief, the next they blazed with cold determination.

Her attention returned to the knights and she watched with interest as Sir Alaric rode towards her. "My Lady Elizabeth, may I accompany you back to the manor? It's a fine day for a walk and it's on my way to Folkingham." He swung his leg over the horse and landed by her side. Bending his head over her hand, he demonstrated that he knew well the chivalric code.

Flattered, she accepted, and together they ambled back towards the manor while Sir Alaric held the horse loosely on a long rein.

Elizabeth was well aware that the estate workers were dissatisfied with the amount of work needed to bring the hay home during the first harvest of the year. The gentlemen farmers demanded that all of the arable land for the manor itself, around thirty per cent of the entire acreage, should be tended first. Only when that was complete would it be followed by the land owned by the tenant farmers. The strips farmed by the bondsmen, the poorest of the villeins, would be harvested last. The cutting commenced amid much muttering and grumbling. The weather was fair but if the rain came before the main group of workers had their own strips cut, then it would be touch and go whether they would get theirs dried and baled in time. The spectre of starvation was always lurking in the background. Fortunately, the clouds stayed away and all was completed in time, much to Elizabeth's relief.

The festivities which traditionally followed the harvest were muted. The manor supplied the usual mead for revelling, and the huge bone fire was lit, fuelled by the burning of animal bones whose pungent aroma warded off evil spirits. However, Elizabeth was aware it lacked the usual rejoicing and dancing. Only a few boys endeavoured to bring themselves good fortune by leaping the flames of the burning cartwheel as it rolled down the shallow hill outside the walls of the manor. The lamb that was let loose among the stubble for any to catch and keep if they could, brought laughing and jeers in equal measure, but it was short-lived when young Billy Weaver flung himself around its neck and held it fast, his to keep and slaughter for his family. While doubtless there would be headaches the next day, from drinking too much, she doubted there would be as many as usual.

As the weeks passed, the second harvest was upon the manor yet again. Lammas Day, on the 1st of August, welcomed the first fruits and grain, and the loaves made from the new wheat were blessed in the church before the main harvest commenced, in the hope of warding off famine.

*

The next day, Elizabeth donned an old hemp dress with an equally aged over-kirtle of linen, a pair of stout boots and a wimple to hold her hair in check. She had determined to help out with the harvest. As they followed the men — who were cutting with their long, two-handled scythes — the women gathered the cut barley before binding the stems and standing the stooks together, ready for the older men to come with the carts to collect them. It was back-breaking work and every so often Elizabeth stood and stretched her aching muscles, hoping the bells of sext would ring soon so they could all stop for refreshment.

At last, seated in the shade of a loaded cart, she collapsed along with the other women, wiping her forehead on her kirtle and taking a swig of weak ale. She closed her eyes against the sun.

"Let's hope Master Reeve, in the absence of a bailiff, will give us leave to work our own strips as well as his." Elizabeth heard the deep voice coming from the group sitting next to another loaded cart. "It was God's good fortune that we were able to harvest our own hay the last time, before the rains came."

It was Master Pullen, who was known for speaking his mind.

"Hush, Peter," said another. "The mistress will hear ye."

"Lady Mary doesn't have any idea what's going on and Lady Elizabeth has sympathy for our troubles."

"It's the manor's privilege to tell us in what order to work. If Master Reeve says do the manor lands first, so be it."

"I only speak the truth."

"Maybe, but at least we have a roof and work, even if it's hard to feed the family."

"Work, yes. Too much of it for too little return. The tithes are too great given what we are expected to do now there's so few of us around to do it."

"Hush! Master Gabriel is just over there. If he hears you…"

Elizabeth opened her eyes as the voice trailed off. She saw another stroll across towards them and recognised the shapely calves beneath the longer cut of the tunic he wore for the harvest. It was Gabriel.

"I understand your grievances, Master Pullen," she heard him say. "I'll speak with my brother. As for the tithes, perchance I have an idea to help solve your concerns, but I must speak with Lady Mary and her children, as I understand they, too, share in the organisation of the manor lands."

"Aye, well, it might help if our strips weren't spread so far apart," said Peter. "We waste time striding between them and having to carry our tools all that way."

"You have a point, but it does ensure that all have a fair distribution of the fertile soil. You know that. If you had more land would you work harder? Or if you had a small increase in wages, perhaps? There is little room for movement in this, I fear, but if it were possible you would need to guarantee some loyalty."

"We might," came the grudging reply.

"I could seek permission to entice some of the Fen folk here from the salt marshes to supplement our number," Gabriel added.

Elizabeth glanced around but the other women were busy wrapping the remains of the cheese and bread into cloths and putting these, along with the flasks of ale, into sacks. None showed any sign of listening in to the men's conversation.

The work continued. It was arduous and at times, seemed never-ending, and ten or eleven bushels for every four roods, once the threshing was complete didn't seem much yield, less for the oats. When the wheat harvest was complete that might be a better return but for every seed sown, to only regain four or five seeds was paltry for all this work. Having to leave one in three fields empty for the soil to recover was frustrating as well. There was no alternative. These thoughts helped Elizabeth to forget the aches in her back.

The bells of the monastery had already chimed the ninth hour when they took a short break for nourishment. Elizabeth distributed damsons to all and some pears from an early fruiting tree in the manor orchard. It was worth it for the good blessings and smiles she received in return.

By the altitude of the sun, she judged the vespers bell would soon be ringing when she saw a man riding towards the manor on a fine-looking horse.

The workers could expect to work for at least another three hours, but Elizabeth's curiosity got the better of her. Returning the borrowed gloves, she made her apologies and promised to return on the morrow before hurrying towards the wooden bridge across the moat.

The horse that stood snorting in the courtyard was being offered a pail of water by a groom, but it was not in the livery of Baron Lord John of Folkingham. As she slipped around the far end of the hall and ran upstairs with all speed to change, the glimpse of a tall figure with wispy hair under a brimmed hat confirmed to Elizabeth that Sir Bartholomew de Ath had come to call on Mary.

CHAPTER 4

"Good day, sir, to what do we owe this visit?" Elizabeth asked with a small curtsey as Sir Bartholomew warmed his backside at the fire in the great hall. Mary was seated nearby.

"Ah, dear child," he said. "What little entertainments have you been about today?" His patronising words grated.

"Sir, I help my mother and brother to run this manor and all its lands. Why, just yesterday I have been out in the fields for the autumn harvest. How goes your own, over towards Sempringham, is it?"

"In that direction but not quite as far. My workers know what's good for them and work hard. I have a reliable reeve and a bailiff who understands exactly what I want. Which brings me to the reason for my visit. I understand from our last meeting, and your mother here assures me I am correct, that you still require a bailiff. I might be able to help you."

Mary looked up at him before inviting him to sit in the chair on the opposite side of the fireplace — Ruadhán's customary seat. Elizabeth gave an involuntary shudder. Sorrow still enveloped her and she took a deep breath as Sir Bartholomew made himself comfortable.

"I'm sure you are aware, dear lady, that the 29th of September is the day for renewing the position of reeve for the following year." He gave an ingratiating smile and glanced briefly at Elizabeth. "I hear your reeve has worked well. Perhaps he might do well as bailiff if you raised him to the position, and you could appoint someone else to the work of reeve on that date."

"You have a great understanding of my circumstances, sir," Mary said, smoothing her dress over her ample figure. "You are most kind. This is all so new and difficult for me." She wound a loose tendril of hair flecked with grey around her finger.

"But not for my brother and I," Elizabeth added quickly. "Rogier will be home very soon, Mother. The decision will be made then. We thank you for your concern, Master de Ath, but all is in hand." She took a small pleasure in the look of irritation that flitted across his face before he mastered his expression.

"Elizabeth, please go to the kitchen and tell them we require refreshment," said Mary. "Master de Ath has ridden a long way on behalf of our solicitude."

As she rose and moved towards the screen shielding the passageway to the kitchens from the hall, Elizabeth heard Mary speak further and lingered.

"Please forgive my daughter, sir. She does not mean to sound so rude. She is young and misses her grandfather."

"I understand my lady. I have a daughter too, and she is only a few months older than yours. Her name is Isabelle and since her mother went to a greater peace with Jesus —" he made the sign of the cross against his chest — "she has been a significant help to me. Our circumstances, mine and yours, are similar, it seems, and I'm sure we may support each other well."

Elizabeth hurried to the kitchens so she might return all the sooner. She distrusted the motivations of this man.

As she re-entered the hall, there was a commotion in the courtyard.

"Oh my!" Mary said. "What now?"

"Have no fear, my lady. I am here," Bartholomew said. "I'm sure I am able to…" His words were drowned out as the heavy oak door flew open and Rogier swept in, bringing the wind with him to disturb the floor rushes.

"I don't have long but I was granted permission to visit. I've had much success at Folkingham. Baron John chose me to help him don his armour in recognition of my proficiency at the tiltyard yester morn." Rogier stopped short as he saw the visitor. "Master de Ath. What brings you to our hearth?"

Before Sir Bartholomew could answer, Elizabeth flew across the floor to greet her brother. "Rogier, how fortuitous that you should arrive at this time," she said, clasping his hand.

Rogier stepped forward and, aware of his training, he greeted Mary and then Sir Bartholomew with appropriate courtliness and asked if refreshments were on their way for their guest.

"Yes, indeed. I have just this minute returned from requesting just that," Elizabeth said. "Master de Ath thinks we need help in appointing a bailiff, Rogier." Then she added pointedly, "Now you are here, perhaps we might do that as soon as our visitor leaves."

"Yes, Sister." Turning to Mary, he said, "Mother, we shall discuss this imminently and act immediately. It's a busy and important season of the year and Marcus Reeve, as well as all the estate workers, need to know what is happening. Now, sir," he turned the discussion with aplomb, "tell us of your ride here. I am interested in the state of fields further away. It has Been decidedly colder these last few years and the harvests have not been good."

"My acres are only five leagues to the north-east. But I agree, the weather has not been favourable for a good yield recently. One or two serfs perished last year —" a puzzled frown flitted over his face before he shrugged — "they said it was shortage of food. I'm not so sure. There are always those who don't work hard. That's why you need a bailiff, sir," he ended with a decisive tone.

"I was discussing the yields with Father Prior at Vaudey. He had information from the records from the Benedictine monks at Norwich Cathedral Priory which substantiates my view. There are extensive records of recent years' growth, sir. The weather is not helping at all, even with those who work hard. Perhaps they need our understanding."

Sir Bartholomew shook his head. "You are young, sir, and perhaps your view will change — with experience. Give them three barleycorns and they'll take a furlong. I know. They will take advantage of you."

This sparring through thinly veiled politeness did not fool Elizabeth and she just managed to stifle a smile when Rogier was able to quote the manorial accounts of St Benet's Abbey near Yarmouth in showing that average temperatures had dropped by nearly one whole degree over a number of years, with yields dropping by almost one third. "Grain prices are rising and making it harder for the poor to feed themselves," he concluded.

Sir Bartholomew must have sensed that he had been bested, for as soon as he had finished his ale and oatcake, he stood to take his leave. "Perhaps we shall meet at the town market one day, dear lady," he said to Mary, who blushed prettily.

"Indeed, sir, and thank you for taking the trouble to visit us."

"As I said before, send a messenger should you need anything at all. Good day to you, Sir Rogier, and Mistress Elizabeth." He gave a perfunctory nod before turning and striding to the door.

Mary and Elizabeth sat in the parlour as Rogier paced. Mary

told him of Sir Bartholomew's suggestion to appoint Marcus Smith as bailiff and then finding a new reeve. However, Rogier agreed with Elizabeth that Marcus could be short with the serfs and villeins, never mind contemplating that they might have grounds for grievances.

"I think Gabriel Smith would make an excellent bailiff," said Elizabeth suddenly. "I heard him speaking just today and he has views in keeping with our own. He understands that since the Great Mortality there is a shortage of people for the work that needs doing. He had ideas to ensure the work of the manor gets done and with ways to supplement the number of people we have to do that. He believes that if there is a small increase in wages, or if villeins have more land of their own, they will work harder with the incentive. He also knows that it's a fine balance."

Rogier looked thoughtful. "And he is familiar with everyone in the manor, so he will be able to cajole or be forceful depending upon to whom he is speaking."

"But Master de Ath suggested we promote Marcus to the position," interrupted Mary. "Oh, it's all so difficult."

"Mother, it's really not," Rogier said. "We must choose who we think best for the position."

"The only concern," continued Elizabeth, "is that Gabriel is a year younger than Marcus, which would mean promoting him above his brother."

"Yes, but the workers will listen to Gabriel. Already Marcus has riled some with his attitude, and I have no doubt that Gabriel can collaborate with his brother," said Rogier.

Mary shrugged. "Whatever you think is best, Rogier. I will leave the decision to you."

The young man looked at his sister, who nodded her enthusiasm for the plan.

*

"Mother and I are intending to visit the market in Stamford,' Elizabeth told Rogier, who was polishing his leather boots. "I need some more spices for the kitchens and Mother is talking of ribbons for the new dress she is sewing."

"It's over an hour's ride in the cart. I suppose Mother would not contemplate taking her own horse and riding," Rogier said without looking up from his boot. Its companion stood to the side of his stool, already with a copper sheen. "I wish I had spurs for these." He sounded wistful.

"All in good time, Rogier. It's a lovely day, why don't you accompany us? We could visit the old coaching inn on the Great North Road, next to the Holy Sepulchre hospital. We could have refreshment there."

Rogier grunted. "You know you only want to gawp at the visitors. It'll be teeming. The religious houses on both sides always ensure that. Anyway, I have no wish to see the Knights of St John of Jerusalem who accompany the pilgrims strutting in the gardens, showing off just because they are on their way to Jerusalem."

"I agree. The Knights Hospitallers ensure it's always busy. We don't need to go to that one — there are other inns in the town. There's one opposite All Saints' Church."

Rogier shook his head. "Not this time. I thought I might go to King John's Tower and work with my horse. Others will be there. You must address household matters with Mother."

Elizabeth was loathe to let him off so easily. "We have made the right choice with Gabriel Smith for bailiff rather than his older brother, have we not?"

Elizabeth reflected on the meeting they had conducted with Gabriel the day before. She remembered his smile at the proposal for the new position and then the suggestions he had put forth for improving things on manor lands. She had determined to be businesslike and not be seduced by his sparkling azure eyes and she had managed, more or less.

"Yes, most definitely," replied Rogier. "How he manages his brother is his concern, but Marcus must go with ease. He knows his position is up for renewal each year. Gabriel is already sounding out a market for the pelts that are lying in the smaller barn, I heard. He will do well. Now I must finish this before I ride across to the tiltyard."

Elizabeth and Mary drove the cart along the route to Stamford. After Edenham village, the track led them up over the hills. With the sun and the birdsong, the light breeze and the green of the trees rustling softly, it was heavenly. Their path descended into the hamlet of Toft where the fields and woods rose high on either side and thence the road was wider and took them towards Stamford town.

The two women entered the walled town by the east gate and left the horse and cart with a man at the stables. They gave him a half groat to provide water and feed, and to maintain the safety of both until their return. Stamford was busy as usual, with market stalls set all the way along the main street. The aroma of a stew cooking in a large skillet and fresh bread assailed their nostrils, and ribbons fluttered from long poles across the front of the stalls.

"We might return here after we have made our purchases," Mary suggested, eyeing the goods on the stalls.

Fruits and vegetables of every shade had been polished to make them more tempting. Rosie beets with the soil still clinging were piled at one end next to carrots and kohlrabi, their green leaves beginning to wilt in the heat. They needed none since their own crops were just as good and very plentiful. They lingered instead at the table of spices, the heady scents filling the air.

"Oh Mother, look, they have some nutmegs." Elizabeth tapped Mary's arm to draw her attention. "We rarely see those. Should we purchase a couple?"

"They're extremely expensive. Well, go on then."

Placing them carefully in her cloth bag along with a screw of saffron and a knobbly stem of ginger, the two women meandered down the hill, stopping occasionally to inspect something of interest.

"Let us find some sustenance before returning up the hill. We can choose the ribbons on the way back," Mary said, brightening at the thought.

There was a commotion towards the bottom of the hill. As they drew closer, they saw two men, naked from the waist up. A crowd were cheering and booing in equal measure as they wrestled; grabbing, spinning, staggering, until eventually one fell with a loud grunt. A cheer arose and the winner strutted in front of them with his arms raised. A third man called, "Whose to try? Come forward. See if you can beat Giant George and win the purse."

A cry went up from the crowd followed by some jeering and jostling as men shoved others forward or encouraged their friends to have a go.

"He certainly looks like a giant," Mary whispered to Elizabeth. "I shouldn't like to cross him. He looks quite fierce. I think we should move away — it's all a little rough."

They were about to leave when Elizabeth heard a man's voice in her ear. He was so close she felt his breath on her skin.

"Are you enjoying the spectacle, ladies? I fear these common men will do almost anything to earn an extra groat, though I suppose they'll probably spend it all in a cheap alehouse."

On seeing Sir Bartholomew, Elizabeth took a step back. "Sir," she said, "you startled me."

The day had lost its glory and a cloud passed over the sun. She shivered.

"You look well, Lady Mary, and the colour of your dress suits you well. Perhaps you would both accompany me for refreshment? The Crown is a respectable establishment. Perhaps a little wine and something to ward off hunger on the return journey. I hear they are selling some fritters sweetened with honey."

Mary's cheeks flushed. "Oh, Sir Bartholomew, that would be lovely." She smiled up at him. "We have still have some ribbons to buy for a new dress I'm making. Elizabeth, hurry back and purchase the lengths we discussed. It will take you no time and you shall meet Master Bartholomew and I in an instant."

Elizabeth was in no hurry to join them and as she wandered back up the hill between the stalls, she delighted in the sights, smells and sounds around her. Two dogs were tussling with a piece of fat which made her chuckle. After buying the ribbons, she retraced her steps.

Upon arriving at the inn, she looked around for Mary and Master Bartholomew but could not see them. There were several small rooms, and she hurried between them, but there was no sign. Eventually, she had a thought. Perhaps they were without, at a table in the small courtyard to the side of the building. As she left by the appropriate door, she saw them seated on the far side. Mary leaned towards Bartholomew, smiling broadly. Gone was her shy flirtatiousness, her more direct response appealing to Sir Bartholomew, since he placed his hand on hers as it rested on the table.

That's a little bold, Elizabeth thought. "Come, Mother, it's getting late and we have a journey of at least four leagues."

Mary sighed but arose. "Sir, it has been my pleasure. Thank you for your hospitality … and your gallantry."

Elizabeth waited impatiently for the pleasantries to pass, before bidding Sir Bartholomew, "Good day, sir."

"I shall do as you say," he said to Mary, before bowing his retreat.

Elizabeth waited until he was out of earshot to enquire his meaning, but Mary was vague in her response. "Oh, he spoke of when we meet again," she said, before hurrying them both towards the stables.

CHAPTER 5

Marcus was red in the face as he paced the tiny living room of the brothers' house. For a moment, Gabriel thought he was going to swipe everything from the table onto the floor. "I am older. I should be bailiff!" he shouted.

"You have a responsible position as reeve and you know the role well. Clearly the Amundevilles d'Albert's think it's too important to move you from that," Gabriel said, trying to placate him.

"Yes, but you won't have to hope they reappoint you every Michaelmas Day. Your position is safe."

"Only as safe as the success with which I do the work, Brother."

"You get accommodation up at the big house." Marcus would not let his grievance pass.

"Only when the family are away, and then you get this place all to yourself. You already get free food and other perks with the position of reeve. It's just a title, Marcus. 'Tis I who will get all the bad-mouthing and upset on each quarter day when it's time to collect the rent and tithes."

Marcus grunted his agreement at this. It was indeed the bailiff who had to suffer the arguments when he asked for cash or kind for his lord, or in this case, Lady Mary and her two children. It was he who must decide which was best for both lady and serf or sokeman. At times of payment to the workers, frequently the serfs would say they needed cash when they were given grain, or tools when they wanted grain. Some were never satisfied and, currently, there was much mumbling and dissatisfaction over the shortage of labour. This was especially so when Marcus dictated the tasks that needed to be done for the manor, like ditch-clearing. Gabriel understood that he would need to employ diplomacy with those he had called friend and he doubted his brother had that skill. His outburst was testament to that.

"Look, I have to go up to the manor to see Lady Mary. I can't be late on my first day and I already heard the bells of prime. If we're not out in the fields we'll be in trouble for sure and we must both set an example now," Gabriel said. Shoving his feet into his boots, he left the house at a pace.

A gentle trot brought him to the wooden bridge across the moat where he paused to admire the old oak wood of the railings, grey and cracked with age, and as his hand touched it he enjoyed the warmth of it, too. At the manor he asked for Lady Mary and was told to wait by the door. The messenger returned, saying, "Lady Mary cannot see you today. She said you must see Lady Elizabeth."

Gabriel sighed. It was important he see someone in authority to verify his plans for the remaining harvest. While he was confident in what needed to be done, he should inform his new employers.

"Lady Elizabeth is already in the fields. You better make shift, Master Smith. The sun is up."

Gabriel turned and made his way to find the daughter of the house. As his boots crunched across the stubble, he heard the swish of the scythes, a constant underlying sibilance as the men called to each other in jest and ribaldry; the women chatting to make the day pass quicker; the children giggling and arguing in turn. All the village were at work together to bring in the precious grains before the weather broke. He turned as he heard a large cart pulled by two oxen, their hooves thudding and their dewlaps swinging in time to their plodding steps as they came towards him. It was the women's job to load it with the stooks which stood drying from the cut several days ago, before trundling back with them to the threshing barn.

He saw Elizabeth in the distance. She was a head taller than most of the women around her, but was included in their lively talk as she bent and stretched in her work. A few chestnut curls escaped from her coif and he grew hot as he watched her move.

By the time he reached her, the wagon was half full. "My lady," he said. "Excuse my intrusion but I went to see your lady mother as requested, but she was unable to see me and it was suggested that I find you. I was going to share my plans for the rest of the harvest and what should be sold, how much dispensed to the workers, and the proportion to be retained by the manor for its own use. Then there is the wood and pelts to discuss. I have found a willing buyer for the skins and thought you should know what I propose for the sale of the timber. That needs to be finalised as soon as possible, since it has stacked up for lack of a bailiff for the last few months."

Elizabeth nodded. "I agree with the situation for the wood. I wondered if it could be shipped to Norwich. There is some major building there, I hear. We need to sit down properly to discuss this. Perhaps you would call at the manor at vespers? By then I shall have returned and changed from this work clothing. I do not believe my lady mother wants to be involved in the running of the lands and my brother is occupied with his knightly training."

Gabriel inclined his head in acknowledgement. "Indeed, my lady."

"Oh come, sir, call me Elizabeth, as you did when we were children running in these very fields."

Gabriel grinned. "Indeed, Elizabeth. I remember we used to play at hide and seek in the woods, too, and on wet days we often met in the barn and practised walking on stilts. I fell off more than you, though. Until vespers." He turned and went to join the men, pulling off his jerkin and undervest as he went and tucking them in his belt. No point getting them hot and dirty unnecessarily. He wondered if Elizabeth's eyes were following him.

The morning wore on, and the wagon was piled high with stooks. Gabriel continued the steady rhythm of swing and cut, swing and cut. He wiped his brow before continuing and glanced at the wagon as it began its path towards the manor barn. The wagon was piled so high its load swayed as it turned. Several children skipped alongside. It was their task to help unload it and, in pairs, stack the stooks in the threshing shed under the watchful guidance of a couple of the older men, one of whom was driving the oxen.

Gabriel continued his work, surreptitiously glancing every so often at Elizabeth.

Elizabeth awaited Gabriel with what she recognised as impatience to see him again, away from the eyes of villagers. She remembered with clarity the youth he had been, tall, gangly, but always fun. The days to which he had referred when they played as children were carefree and they had laughed a great deal.

Now, she couldn't help but be flattered by the look in his eyes and as a result had dressed carefully, choosing colours that complemented her, and pulling a few strands of hair from her coif to fall against her cheeks. When he arrived, they would go into the parlour. She didn't need a scribe, being fully conversant with reading, writing and numbers, and she prayed this would not intimidate for him. While she waited, she thought of Clémence and was grateful, once again, for the schooling upon which her beloved grandmother had insisted.

Upon his arrival, Elizabeth gestured for Gabriel to sit opposite her at the small table in the parlour. Sitting side-by-side would have been easier to look at the figures on the parchment and she regretted, too late, the arrangement. And why this tension between them when there was camaraderie in the fields earlier? Surely she had caused it by this positioning, unwittingly making it plain that as the daughter of the manor she was above him, socially. Perhaps she could invite him to her side of the table. She dithered but it was too late now. She made a show of settling into her seat to cover her indecision.

After studying, in detail, the figures on the parchment, she initiated the discussion about the timber before Gabriel shared his arrangements for the pelts and ideas regarding the harvest. As she glanced across at him, she saw his eyes sparkle as they watched her with intensity. She looked down in haste at the parchment, but secretly hoped his look was one of admiration.

Gabriel sat where Elizabeth suggested and smiled inwardly as he observed her fluster and then her desperation to appear efficient and knowledgeable. Her ideas for the wood were along the same lines as his. As she concentrated on the lists and prices before her, shallow lines creased her forehead. Of all the women he knew she was the fairest to behold, and when she looked up and caught his eyes upon her he took some deep breaths to calm his heart. He recalled the words he had read from a work by Guillaume de Palerne. The author had been writing for the Countess Yolande of Hainault, but Gabriel had seen a version in the poetic form of alliterative verse, having come across the manuscript while in the monastery library. He was curious to see it before it disappeared to the library in Cambridge. He kept such visits to himself. His contemporaries wouldn't understand his craving for knowledge, and would only jest at his expense.

Gabriel cleared his throat, resisting the urge to make the sign of the cross. As it was, he would have to confess his irreverent thoughts about Lady Elizabeth the next time he went to confession, although he would not name her. He dragged his attention back to the discussion. He sat up straight and started to speak. Elizabeth listened with attention to his ideas and approved them all.

When they parted they each had a deeper astuteness of the other, and also a deeper regard.

Elizabeth was in dire need of something to expel the stiffness that had crept upon her and in casting about for ideas of an activity, she had a thought and went in search of Rogier. There was still almost three hours of daylight left and the practise yard at King John's Tower would not be busy. She knocked on the door to his solar and, hearing Rogier's voice, she entered. "Brother, what say we go to the tiltyard at the tower?"

"Now? Not likely. I've been busy all day." This was as she expected.

"You remember how we used to practise as children? With our wooden staves?"

"I do. In the orchard or on the fallow fields."

"May I borrow some of your things? I shall be most careful and return them all in good form."

At this, Rogier sat upright. "You jest?"

"Not at all. I will be ready should there be trouble in the future. You never know what may come. I could be of use if I know what I'm about and have practised, and I fancy some diversion, right now. I've been working on manor business all day, while you've been out. We could both go if you do not trust me, but you know I am perfectly capable of riding a horse and I see that you are resting." She glanced at the wine cup next to him. "I wouldn't take your plate armour, just some clothes and perhaps the mail suit?"

"You most certainly will not take my plate. When it was gifted to me by Ruadhán it was not to be shared recklessly. It cost a fortune." He paused and took a swig from his cup. "Oh, go on then. You may borrow my clothes and the mail, if you think you have the strength to bear its weight."

Elizabeth leaped forwards and kissed his cheek.

"Get off, you soft thing." He shrugged her away, a brother's typical reply.

Elizabeth grabbed a jerkin, a belt, and some leggings, calling over her shoulder as she hurried out of the door, "Thank you, dear brother." Before he had time to change his mind she had disappeared behind her own door to change into his clothing.

Nobody gave her a second look as she left the armourer's room dressed in Rogier's mail, a scarf around her lower face and his helm upon her head covering the cloth she had wound around her hair. To all intents it could have been Rogier mounting a horse in the courtyard and riding out across the wooden bridge, so alike in height were they. Her laughter rang out as she rode with all speed to King John's Tower up on the hill.

Upon arrival she dismounted and looked around. A few young men were on the far side of the arena. It looked like they were practising some of the seven points of agility, the physical skills a knight was expected to master. Two were fencing, one was shooting arrows at a target, while two others were wrestling. Elizabeth fancied a fast ride at a quintain or the quoits. She wanted to feel the wind in her face and to prove success to herself in the art of knightly activity. She missed sitting astride a horse, feeling its muscles ripple as she galloped with a purpose, now that she was a young woman and expected to deal with household chores and the daily management of the manor. She glanced around. The other men were busy and paying her no attention. She was simply another young squire in training.

Pulling a short training lance from the stands, she took her position to pierce the small ring which dangled from an arm hanging across her path with her weapon, and encouraged the horse forwards. Her first run was a disaster, since she missed it spectacularly, only proving to herself that this activity of ring-running was long overdue. The boy had no need to rehang the small target and she was sure the look he gave her was one of puzzlement.

Elizabeth reined the horse around and kicked with her heels, it sprung forwards again. This time she had greater success and, throwing back her head, she gave a great whoop.

"Do you want them again, my lord?" asked the boy.

Elizabeth nodded. Her third run was a success and having fulfilled her mission she passed the boy the lance, nodded her thanks and turned for home. As she reached the end of the run, the sound of hooves behind her made her half-turn.

"Are you coming for a wrestle, Rogier?" a voice she recognised asked. Her stomach clenched. It was Sir Alaric.

"No." Elizabeth lowered her voice. She was pleased the scarf hid her lower face and she dropped her chin to ensure he didn't recognise her eyes. "I'm leaving. A mild imbalance of the humours."

"Ah! You best get home then." His horse stepped back as he pulled the reins. Everyone feared illness.

"I'll be fine by the morrow. 'Tis nothing serious." The thought of wrestling with Alaric nearly made Elizabeth chuckle and she had to bite her lip.

"Until tomorrow then," said Sir Alaric. "Give my regards to that fair sister of yours."

Elizabeth waved as she rode off. She hadn't gone far when she pulled the scarf from her mouth so that she could laugh uproariously at her deception.

CHAPTER 6

The next day followed the same pattern as the others. Before the prime bells and with the rising sun, as many people as were healthy were out in the fields. The cutting of the rye and barley were done and the stooks taken on the cart to the barns ready for threshing and grinding. The harvest of the wheat and oats was under way, and the women had gathered the grain stalks into bundles as thick as a man's waist. After binding them they propped them together to await the wagon. The steady rhythm of the scythes, so much more efficient than the old-fashioned sickles, continued with the men swinging in unison, their swish, swish was a constant undertone to all else.

Marcus kept a keen eye on the workers as he leant a hand. If there was any suggestion of shirking, he was ready with a curse and a threatening word. As it was, he'd already had a sharp word for Martha Baker. Elizabeth noticed that she lagged behind as they all moved forward across the field.

"Are you ailing, Martha?"

"A little, my lady. I believe I may be with child again. I hope it's a boy this time. I did everything just as Old Mother Hubb in the village did tell me. I clenched my fists while my husband performed nature's act, and I told him he must face east, too. That should ensure success. And look, I'm stepping with my right foot first. Oh, but I have been so ill in the mornings, and have such a cissa," Martha said, using the village word for her food craving.

"And what is it that you desire so much?"

"Milk, my lady. The cow's first squirt each morning and eve. I cannot get enough."

"It will be the babe telling you what it needs," said Elizabeth.

"Do you think so? I have not held one this long before, so I wasn't certain."

"I'm sure all will be well, Martha."

"Perhaps I'll ask Master Reeve if I might accompany the wagon and help the children to unload it. Would that be permissible, my lady?"

"I'm sure it would. Tell him I think your vigilance over the young ones will speed the process."

"Thank you, my lady."

It took an age before the wagon was finally laden. Piled high, it turned on its shaky path and trundled away while the next came forward in line to take its turn. The field was rutted now with previous journeys, the hefty wooden wheels leaving deep tracks, the soil pitted by oxen hooves. The women stood, hands on hips, arching their backs to give muscles a chance to stretch while the next wagon came level and before they started to load the bundles. It was dusty work and Elizabeth wiped the back of a gloved hand across her forehead.

Having watched the load on its way, she returned to the line to gather the next pile for tying and standing in its group with the others before loading. Without warning, there was a cry followed by a loud cracking of wood and a piercing scream. All the workers turned. Then they began to run. Some of the women reached the overturned cart before the men, since they were further away across the field.

As they sped cross the treacherous ground, more than one person turned an ankle and another fell face-first, spreadeagled across the ground. Their sights were on reaching the wreckage ahead.

It was a gruesome sight. The wagon driver, an elderly serf, lay groaning. He had been thrown to the ground, his head bleeding and one leg twisted at an unnatural angle.

"Run for the doctor, Master Butcher," Marcus called. "Old William will need this leg binding. It looks like a broken bone."

"Or lopping," someone muttered.

Some of the men began to investigate the damage to the wagon. It was a costly accident.

"A new wheel, of course," one said.

Another pointed at the underside of the vehicle. "Aye, and the central reach is splintered, as well as the axle. Completely shattered, see?"

"The old fool must have been going too fast. Lady Mary won't want to pay for all this."

"Stop gossiping like goodwives and get this lot stacked ready for another wagon," Marcus called.

A collective gasp arose as they lifted the first few bundles of fallen stooks.

"God's teeth."

"Dear Lord!"

Elizabeth hurried round to see what had caused such consternation and fell to her knees to cradle the head of Martha Baker. Blood was pumping from a wound to the woman's neck, seeping into the earth and the fabric of Elizabeth's kirtle. There was nothing she could do and Martha breathed her last breath.

Tears sprang to Elizabeth's eyes. "We were talking not one hour ago. She told me she was expecting another child. Where is Master Baker?" She looked up at the faces around her.

A young man pushed through the crowd and Elizabeth moved out of the way as he dropped to his knees and scooped the lifeless body of his wife onto his lap. He swayed and groaned, his grief raw for all to see.

All who witnessed, watched with awkward sorrow.

When Old William and the body of Martha Baker had been carted away, Marcus spoke. "We're two workers down now. I expect you all here tomorrow as usual, including you, Master Baker."

Elizabeth was shocked. "A little sensitivity would go a long way, Master Reeve," she spoke quietly to him before dragging her weary body and aching feet back to the manor house.

When she arrived, the last person she expected to find was Master Bartholomew de Ath with Mary. She greeted him politely and then took the opportunity to go to her rooms and bathe before changing out of her workaday clothing. Upon her return, Sir Bartholomew was taking his leave. It was already late, being well past vespers. Soon the sun would disappear and the bells for compline would ring.

"I look forward to our next meeting, my dear Lady Mary," he said.

"I too, sir," Mary replied, and then in an undertone, "I shall not be late." Elizabeth was unsure if she had heard right but when she questioned her mother, Mary was brusque and told her to mind her own affairs. This piqued Elizabeth's curiosity even more and she determined to speak with Rogier at the next opportunity.

The following day the atmosphere in the fields was subdued. Elizabeth caught Master Baker glaring at Marcus on more than one occasion and during their mid-morning break there was much whispering among the male serfs. At the end of this lull from work several of them approached Marcus.

"Sir, we would crave a word," said Master Baker.

"Make it quick. You have duties awaiting," said the reeve.

"Father Bernard said we must bury Martha before sext tomorrow, for he must be at Sempringham for another service by noon. As you know, sir, we dare not leave it another day."

Another pleaded the case for Master Baker. "Aye, Old Mother Hubb has cleaned and laid her down. She lies wrapped in her shroud and awaits her final journey. She must not wait, sir, or her time in Purgatory will be all the longer."

Marcus sighed. "Very well, but only you two may attend. You others have work owed to the manor." He waved his hand around those gathered.

Elizabeth thought it wise not to intervene, aware that Marcus's self-esteem had already been dented following the appointment of his younger brother to the more senior position of bailiff. The last thing he needed was for her to undermine his authority now.

Shortly after the midday break, Marcus eyed some white clouds which had bubbled up to the west. He pointed. "The weather may break any day. Look up yonder — clouds are forming. Get to work. Who knows how many days we have and I want these oats in the barn."

They were all hard at work when Elizabeth looked up and saw Mary's carriage leaving the manor. She was too far away to hail and enquire where she was heading, though she thought she saw a flash of iridescent blue silk.

Mother is wearing her best gown, she thought. She must be meeting someone of note to be dressed in her finery. Something stirred in the pit of her stomach. Yester eve, Mary had reassured Sir Batholomew that she would not be late. Was she meeting him for some reason? And if so, why go alone and not take one of the maids? If only Rogier was at home. He could have accompanied their mother, or at least discovered her business.

Gabriel appeared in the field and all thoughts of Mary vanished. As she stared at his dark curls and broad shoulders, gone were the memories of shared childhood games and in their place … oh! Heat rose to her face and Elizabeth mentally shook herself. He was not for her. She would be married by the whim of Lord John, no doubt, and not to a bailiff. She turned her mind to the unrest among the workers and decided to confide in Gabriel about it.

"I fear the accident has given weight to the grievances of the serfs and villeins, sir," she said. "They mutter among themselves. There was a suggestion that the wagon was overloaded to save time."

"I have heard as much. I'm not sure my brother realises the fine line we tread at the moment."

Elizabeth was worried. "What do you suggest?"

"Perhaps I might have leave to ride to Hagbeach. It's about two hours ride from here. I understand there is a manor in that part of the Fens that has lost its lord and the villagers are dispersing regardless of permissions. Perhaps some may come here and work for us. In exchange for the usual tithes, we would care for them as we do our own with accommodation and the promise of safety."

"It is certainly people that we need. Perhaps you should make haste. Others will be offering the same and we may be too late."

"I have hesitated to suggest it before. There is a poorer side to the idea."

"What might that be?"

"Would our own people accept the presence of strangers? It would bode ill should they not, my lady."

"In what way?" she asked.

Gabriel frowned. "They may say their bread is being taken from their mouths by strangers. They may resent the presence of people coming and living in the houses previously occupied by their own."

"It cannot be both ways," said Elizabeth. "Either they are overworked or we seek help for them."

"This is true. So, shall I proceed?"

"I wish my brother were here, that I might consult him, too. My mother shows little interest and her mind flits from one thing to another in as many seconds."

Gabriel did not comment. It wasn't his place to criticise the lords and ladies of the manor.

Elizabeth realised his discomfort. "I know you will say naught but 'tis true ... and please, call me Elizabeth."

Gabriel grinned at her and the old camaraderie was reestablished.

Elizabeth thought for a few moments before reaching a decision. "Yes, go and enquire. But ensure they understand they will receive no more than our own people. Do not bargain. Take the rest of the day and report back to me. Once we know the facts, we will be better able to decide how many workers we can take and whether they bring families or not."

Gabriel nodded. "I agree. They come on our terms or not at all. Before I go, perhaps I may speak with our three most reliable sokemen to explain the situation. That way they will align with us and help to persuade any who speak against the idea."

"Indeed. Do that, then make haste. As soon as you return, we will make the final decision and move forwards with speed."

Elizabeth watched him gather Marcus and Masters Miller, Smith and Oates. They stood in a huddle as Gabriel spoke to them. She watched their reactions with a keen eye and was relieved when the older men nodded. Marcus shrugged and said nothing. Gabriel turned and gave her a wave before hurrying off to the manor. It wasn't long before she saw him riding a Paso Fino horse, bred by her father from a pair he had bought on the Spanish border when he was engaged on the continent. Its energy and endurance as well as fleetness of foot was an asset. It was a sensible choice of mount, expressing Gabriel's seniority, which was essential to demonstrate to the unknown workers that his proposal had credence.

Gabriel rode with all speed, pleased he had a sturdy and reliable mount, but it was still a two-hour journey. As he travelled, the landscape altered from soft, undulating ground to flat, marshy areas. In one place he saw the more familiar pattern of strip farming on high ground where the land was arable.

Once or twice he passed salterns, evidence of ancient reclamation of salt from the tidal waterways, and once he passed an area where steam rose from huge vats, the evaporation of seawater leaving behind the valuable salt. Gabriel's natural curiosity was keen to learn more about the process, but he was aware of time passing and his mission. He stopped a man cutting peat to ask his way to Hagbeach and was told it was only a short ride.

As he approached his destination, he saw the land rise slightly. The task ahead was sensitive but he would not be daunted. He would find out if the local people were interested in moving and ensure his proposal was stated with clarity and decisiveness, being sure to let them know he would return with all speed to finalise an agreement.

Elizabeth watched the sun's path and was relieved as it slowly sank. All day her thoughts had flicked between Mary's whereabouts and how Gabriel's progress was going. Eventually she heard the sound of hooves on the road and looked across the expanse of stubble. It was her mother's carriage, but a man on a horse accompanied it. Master Batholomew de Ath sat proud upon a fine horse, turning his head this way and that, surveying all he passed.

CHAPTER 7

Master de Ath stood by the fire, his hand resting on the mantel and his foot up on the fender, looking for all the world as if he owned the place. Opposite Mary, who sat in her customary chair to one side, was a young woman, near to Elizabeth's own age, she judged. She wore a gown of pale blue linen. Her skin was pale, too, and a few strands of hair were curled artfully around her face. She sat demurely with her hands clasped in her lap. When Elizabeth drew near, she glanced up but did not smile.

"Mother." Elizabeth bobbed a curtsey before her. "Master de Ath." She inclined her head before nodding to the younger woman. "I do not think we have met, mistress."

"I am Isabelle de Ath and this is my father. I am pleased to be here."

Elizabeth glanced at Mary, who seemed nervous and looked to Sir Bartholomew. He said nothing but stared at Elizabeth. She did not like the boldness of his gaze.

Mary cleared her throat. "We have … news to impart." She twisted her fingers in her lap. "I've been meaning to tell you, to discuss with you…" Mary trailed off and looked again at Sir Bartholomew. "You explain, sir," she said to him.

"If you wish, my dear," he said.

My dear? Elizabeth's eyes widened.

"'Tis merely this," he said. "We have indeed news and pleasant it is, I'm sure you will agree. Today, your mother is no longer alone in the world and unhappy with her estate."

Elizabeth's throat was suddenly dry. "I … I don't understand."

"It's simple enough. This day, your mother has done me the honour of accepting my hand and we have tied the nuptial knot. I am now your stepfather, and Isabelle here becomes your sister. I am the new master of Grimsthorpe manor."

Mary turned to Elizabeth. "We could not manage as we were with Rogier away so frequently and still a boy really. There is a complexity to running the manor and we needed a good man to look after our affairs."

Elizabeth finally found her voice. "I cannot believe it. You have married this man? What of the memory of my father? And what of Ruadhán and Clémence? Is this how they would wish the manor to move forwards? To hand all that we have worked for to this … this man?"

"How dare you speak thus to your mother?" growled Bartholomew. "You will welcome your new sister and apologise to your mother."

"Elizabeth is headstrong," Mary said, tears shimmering on her lashes. "She and Rogier think they run the manor."

"And with the help of our new bailiff we are making good work of it." Elizabeth was aware her voice was rising and spoke her next words quietly and with menace. "You are *not* master of this manor, sir. Lord Amundeville, my grandfather and knight of the realm, left my brother Rogier and I to manage the estate. I shall *never* call you father." She turned and strode across the rush-covered floor of the great hall and up the staircase. Slamming the door of her solar, she flung herself onto the bed, where bitter tears came. She could only imagine what Rogier would say. She beat her fist upon the cushions in impotent fury at the deed already done.

Time passed and dusk crept through the window before she heard footsteps on the wooden stairs. The door to Mary's room next door opened and closed. Elizabeth lay on her bed and didn't move. She heard voices.

"Wife, the girl is in need of discipline to be sure. A good whipping will bring her into line. She has forgotten her place."

She heard Mary's breathy voice. "Oh sir, she means no harm, I am sure. Our news came as a shock to her, that is all. If she but has a little time, I'm certain she will come around. Her father, my husband, never had cause to take a whip to her."

"I am your husband now, Mary, and Elizabeth must learn to obey me. She is too wilful but that will soon change. And now, Wife, we have matters to see to that are private between a man and his new spouse."

"But sir, dinner will soon be served. I asked the staff to prepare something special for us."

"Remove your clothing and kneel before me. I am your husband and I shall have some delight. Do as I say. Now!"

Elizabeth clapped her hands over her ears. She wanted to hear no more. She contemplated what she should do. Rogier needed to know and the sooner the better. She determined to ride to the castle and take word to him. She could not delay — she would ride there this very night. Her brother's clothes were still in her chest, and she could hide her hair under the hood of a jerkin. As she changed her clothing, Elizabeth tried not to listen to the sounds from the next room. Was that crying she could hear?

The evening air was cool as Elizabeth rode with all haste to Folkingham Castle. She had been before with her family as guests of Sir John, 4th Lord Beaumont and his lady, Katherine, but the last time had been the funeral and laying to rest of her grandfather, Ruadhán. The baron had many important duties, and his work for the Crown meant he was often absent from his country home and she hadn't seen Lady Katherine during that last sorrowful visit since she was expecting the birth of a child. She might well be there now, following the birth of their son, Lord Henry.

As she approached the castle a guard at the gate stopped her. "Dismount and approach, boy. What is your business here at this hour?"

Elizabeth's mouth dried as she realised that she had fled the manor without a clear plan and that it had been foolish to ride out so late. She cleared her throat and said, "I come with an important message for my b... for Sir Rogier Amundeville d'Albert.

"And what might this important message be?"

"It is for his ears alone. Let me pass." As soon as she spoke, Elizabeth regretted her haughty tone. Now she would never gain entry.

The guard frowned. "Messages should be told to the officer of the guard first — that's me, Peter Parry — so I will judge the importance."

Thinking better of her mission, Elizabeth turned to leave. It could await until tomorrow, when she would return properly dressed and in full daylight. Before she could mount her horse, however, Parry grabbed her wrist and thrust his pudgy face in hers. She drew back from the stench of his breath.

"Let me go this minute!" she demanded, straightening to her full height.

He pulled her closer. "Ah, so it's a maid we have with all her soft roundness, and not a lad at all. I'm not sure if Sir Rogier is within. He may be out on patrol or up at King John's Tower." He grinned, revealing rotten teeth. He turned to a companion who sat beside a nearby brazier. "Cut along and find out if Sir Rogier is within."

Elizabeth watched as the younger man ran across the drawbridge.

"I reckon we might amuse ourselves while we wait and you can tell me why you wear this disguise. After all, I could report you to the churchmen and then you would be arrested. I'm sure the sumptuary laws don't allow such trickery. Perhaps share with me what it is you were going to share with Sir Rogier." Parry leered at her and licked his lips. "Come this way, my dear."

Elizabeth wrenched her wrist free and took a step back. "I'll wait here."

"My, you are a proud one, aren't you? Dressed as a boy you might be, but I could teach you a thing or two, sweet maid."

Quick as a diving falcon his arm shot out around her waist, pulling her to him once more, and she felt the hardness of his body. For one moment she thought he was going to place his mouth on hers, but as it was, his other hand reached the neck of her shirt and wrenched. She heard the fabric rip as his hand groped for her breast. Elizabeth cried out before a determination from deep within arose. She lifted her knee with all her force and rammed it into his groin. Parry instantly released her with a curse to the Almighty as he rolled on the ground, gasping.

Without hesitation, Elizabeth ran as fast as her legs would carry her, over the bridge and into the outer courtyard of the castle, heedless of whether she was allowed there. Her only thought was to get away, for she was certain that if Parry found her again, there would be no release and his revenge would be brutal.

Elizabeth stood on the cobbles, clutching the torn fabric of her clothing and looking around, desperately wondering how she would find Rogier and hoping that she wouldn't meet anyone of note. It was impossible to return the way she had come, though her horse was there, somewhere. Her situation was dire and if she had forfeited the animal there would be further trouble at home. It was valuable. She berated herself for having been so impetuous.

As she hesitated, a door opened and two ladies emerged from the gardens beyond. One was older but the younger was Lady Katherine, Baroness Beaumont. She was younger than Elizabeth by almost two years, and six years younger than her husband, who she had married the year before. The two women were laughing as they entered the courtyard. Elizabeth had nowhere to hide and when Lady Katherine saw her she straightened.

"Who is that bedraggled youth? Come before me and explain yourself." Lady Katherine's voice was imperious and used to being obeyed.

Elizabeth moved towards the pair and curtseyed. "My lady. I apologise for my attire."

"You appear to have had some misfortune. Move over here so I might see your face."

Elizabeth moved towards the light of a torch that blazed in a sconce on the wall.

"Oh! I know you, do I not?" The sheen of rich fabric and intricate stitching on the borders of her sleeves, neckline and hem, reserved for ladies of her class, caught in the light.

Elizabeth clutched at her torn shirt. "I apologise, my lady. I am Lady Elizabeth Amundeville d'Albert come with a message for my brother Sir Rogier. I am dressed in his clothes because, well … I … I sought to come in haste, hence my disguise at this late hour."

Lady Katherine frowned. "Disguise? Why should that be necessary?"

"Forgive me, my lady. The message I have for my brother is a family matter and I wished to leave the manor…" She hesitated, wondering how best to explain. "To leave the manor without the knowledge of my new stepfather."

"I see," said Lady Katherine, though from her expression it was clear that she didn't understand at all. "You are the daughter of Mistress Mary Amundeville d'Albert and granddaughter of the famed Sir Ruadhán and Lady Clémence Amundeville, are you not? You best tell me what happened to cause the disarray to your clothing."

Again, Elizabeth hesitated, but realised the lady's tone of voice would brook no evasion. "It was one of the guards at the gate, my lady."

"He laid his hands upon you? Did you provoke him in some way?"

"Provoke him!" Elizabeth responded with deep indignation. "If you mean did I encourage him to maul me and tear my clothing, no, my lady, I certainly did not!"

Lady Katherine sighed and shrugged. "It seems no real harm is done." She turned to her companion. "Tell the man at the door to find Sir Rogier and send him to await my presence in the attendance room. Then take Mistress Elizabeth to find some suitable clothing into which she might change. I shall arrive shortly." She looked directly at Elizabeth. "We shall speak more in a little while."

"Yes, my lady. Thank you." Elizabeth followed the older woman towards the inner courtyard and the door to the castle's great hall.

As she entered she glanced around, admiring the silver plate on the table, the tapestries that adorned the walls. This was the country home of one of the leading knights of the realm, who had the ear of the king and who dealt with matters of state.

Elizabeth was taken aloft and passed to a servant who was instructed to find her a suitable gown. When it came it was of fine russet linen and she was shown to a bowl of water where she could rinse her face and hands. She rewound her hair and used the length of cream linen to cover it in a coif before she was led up a spiral staircase and onwards to a dark oak door. The maid knocked and then nodded for Elizabeth to enter the oblong anteroom where a fire burned with leaping flames, for although it was still late summer, the evenings were chilly within the thick castle walls. Tapestries hung from the stone walls and a rich-coloured rug from the Middle East covered the rushes, which were scented with lavender. Two sturdy oak chairs were placed either side of the fireplace and in one sat her brother.

"Rogier!" Elizabeth hurried across to greet him with a sigh of relief.

"Sister, what on earth are you doing here?"

Elizabeth told him of the occurrence at the gate.

"Christ's toenails!" Rogier swore. "I'll have the brute's entrails strung up for the crows to devour."

"No, Rogier. You must not get into a fight on my account. I doubt I shall see him again. Forget him. He is of little importance. Listen, I came to give you news."

"At this time of night? What could be so important? Is Mother unwell?"

"It is Mother, but she is well. This morning, Rogier, she went to Stamford town and she took a husband."

Rogier frowned. "What? She is married? I don't understand. There was no word when last we met."

"None of us knew. But Rogier, that is not the worst of it." Elizabeth took a deep breath. "Her new husband is none other than Bartholomew de Ath."

Rogier's jaw dropped. "You jest, Sister. That ... that creeping, obsequious little man. That money-grabbing crawler?"

"I hardly dared tell you. He will rule our manor now, and I fear it will not be with wisdom and sensitivity."

Rogier paced the room, his fists clenched. "I'll have his head if he takes my inheritance. Our grandfather left me the manor as my birthright, and for us to run the estate, knowing Mother did not have the aptitude or wish for it. Well, let's see how she likes living next door to the pigs and sheep on some farm near Sempringham with her new husband."

"Rogier, you cannot mean... Ruadhán intended us to care for Mother. We cannot send her away. I know you're angry, but you must not do anything that we would all regret. We will work around this," Elizabeth said, then, more quietly, "somehow."

Before Rogier could say more, the curtains parted at the far end of the room and Lady Katherine appeared. She had changed from her gown of blue to one of deep red and rubies glowed on her earlobes. A heavy gold cross hung between her breasts and her dark hair was twisted with gold thread and wound around her head in the new Italian fashion. Young she might be, but she was clearly the lady of this castle. Both Elizabeth and Rogier immediately showed their obeisance with deep deference. "Thank you, my lady, for these clothes," said Elizabeth.

"I do not need them back." When brother and sister straightened, Lady Katherine remarked with surprise, "Goodness, now I see you together you are very alike."

"Many have said the same, my lady," said Rogier. "Elizabeth has been known to wear my clothes in the fields of the manor and people have oft mistaken her for me."

"She was wearing your clothes when I found her earlier," commented Lady Katherine.

"Some think we are twins, but we are only close in age," added Elizabeth hastily, not wishing to aggravate her brother's temper again.

"You better accompany your sister home, Rogier. It is dark and getting late. In view of her mishap earlier, I think it would be wise, and in my husband's absence, I give permission. Return after daylight tomorrow."

"Thank you, Katherine," Rogier said.

Elizabeth was surprised at the familiarity. And was that a wink? God forbid he was overstepping. She determined to question him about their relationship later, fearing that Rogier was getting into deep water. They would all suffer if 'twere thus.

As they left the castle precincts and headed towards the bridge, Sir Alaric was passing through the outer courtyard. Elizabeth greeted him but neither she nor Rogier stopped to talk. She was aware of his gaze as she glanced over her shoulder, but she needed to retrieve her mount. She was increasingly concerned it may have wandered.

Brother and sister headed to the gatehouse at the end of the long drive. Peter Parry was nowhere in sight but the second guard showed them where he had hobbled the horse, which was patiently cropping grass nearby.

As they rode away Rogier said, "I shall be having a few words when we return to the manor."

"Please, Brother," replied Elizabeth, "do not say anything that we may all regret later. What is done cannot be undone."

CHAPTER 8

On arriving in the great hall, Rogier turned to Elizabeth. "Wait here," he said, then turned and took the stairs two at a time.

Elizabeth sat with her embroidery in her hand but made no stitches as she heard a sharp rap on the door of her mother's bedchamber. "Come out at once the pair of you for I would speak with you."

Elizabeth gasped. Surely no good would come from the upset. The deed was done and she could manage Master Bartholomew, surely. Yet, as she had these thoughts she felt, deep down, that he could not be trusted.

"Come out, both of you," Rogier repeated when there was no response. "Or do I have to enter?"

A high-pitched exclamation from inside the chamber could be heard all the way downstairs and Elizabeth imagined Mary's fear and upset.

A small group of workers who had been bedding down for the night on their pallets at the far end of the great hall had roused themselves. Elizabeth was aware of their whispers and gasps of shock. Nothing like this had happened during their tenure.

Elizabeth climbed a few steps so she might see the door to the chamber above. Several moments passed before it opened and Bartholomew de Ath appeared, holding a candle and dressed in a white nightshirt and cap. His face was red, though whether this was surprise or anger, Elizabeth knew not. At his shoulder stood a pale-faced Mary, clutching her nightgown at her neck.

"You listen to me, boy —" began Bartholomew, thrusting the door wide in a display of force. He stopped short as Rogier took a step forward, his palm on the hilt of the dagger at his belt. His fingers curled around the tang.

"No, sir, you listen to me," Rogier said, his voice deep with authority. "My mother may have chosen to throw herself upon your mercy but it done without my permission, and I am her guardian. My grandfather, Sir Ruadhán Amundeville, made that clear before he passed. However, you have been crafty enough to tie the nuptial knot with speed, and it cannot be undone. But hear this and pay attention well. This manor is mine. It is my birthright and the same noble knight who gave me guardianship of my mother gave me the right to decide how it should be managed. In my absence, my sister Elizabeth was given the right to govern and you will live here with our toleration only. You will alter nothing without our agreement."

Elizabeth's heart was beating hard as she listened to Rogier's words. She realised he had grown into a man with all the authority of the knight he was soon to be.

"Why, you … you young…" Sir Bartholomew could not finish his sentence, so suffused was he with rage. Behind him, Mary whimpered.

"Think well as you act, Master de Ath. I shall not give further notice!" With these words Rogier turned and strode towards the staircase as Bartholomew, his eyes bulging, disappeared back inside the bedchamber, the door slamming.

Elizabeth head a small cry and the sounds of anguish coming from the bedchamber. Her instinct was to go to Mary, but that was made impossible with Master de Ath residing within the room.

"Elizabeth, descend with me," Rogier said, and then he bade the company at the foot of the stairs to withdraw. She saw them scuttle away to their straw-filled pallets as she accompanied her brother to the fire at the other end of the hall.

"I have never been so angry," Rogier said as he flung himself into the chair in which his grandfather used to sit. "I must return to the castle tomorrow. Best you speak with Gabriel and apprise him of the situation. I would do that, but you heard what Lady Katherine said — I must return at first light. There is a tourney to finish planning and guests to invite in honour of the first anniversary of the marriage of my lady and her sire."

"Indeed, I shall do that." Elizabeth paused, wondering how best to ask him about his relationship with Lady Katherine, but then Rogier continued.

"Tell Gabriel the full thrust of what I said to Bartholomew. Ensure he knows to listen to you and not to him. I think I shall retire for the night, I am exhausted."

With these words he was gone and Elizabeth realised she would have to wait until the morning to question him about his friendship with Lady Katherine.

Elizabeth awoke to the bells of terce. Realising that she had overslept, she leapt from her bed, splashed water on her face with haste, and donned the same dress given to her by Lady Katherine. She descended the staircase only to discover that Rogier had left much earlier. Her questions would have to wait, though surely he would have more sense than to be over-friendly with the wife of his sponsor.

Mary and Bartholomew were also nowhere to be seen that morning, probably still within the bedchamber. Elizabeth shuddered at the thought. She was relived not to face them and decided to find Gabriel and speak with him. She began her search at the stables and then proceeded to the forge and the orchard. She should have known he would be helping in the fields and gone straight there. As she approached the men cutting the last of the oats she recognised Gabriel by his height. As she approached, she called him by name. Clearly it was hot, dusty work and he wiped his face on the hem of his shirt before picking up his cotehardie and pulling it on as he walked towards her.

"Good day, Elizabeth," he said.

"Gabriel, I would speak with you. Perhaps we might find somewhere quiet where ears will not listen and eyes will not guard us."

"The orchard is cool and few will be there at this time of the year. That work will not commence for another month or two." His voice took on an excited tone. "I have a new and ready market for the surplus wood that we spoke of before. I have been asking around and there is a sawmill over towards Corby Glen."

"Thank you, we shall discuss that and I do want to hear how the men from Hagbeach will be accepted. I know they will come with all speed, glad of the opportunity, but will they been well-received? There are so many perils to overcome with the notion."

"The sokemen are making the reason for them coming quite plain, so with God's grace all will be peaceful." Gabriel gave her an understanding smile full of gentle understanding for her concern.

Elizabeth was relieved. "Perhaps we might discuss the wood in a while, but at this moment I must share with you a matter concerning my mother and the manor."

Gabriel looked across at Elizabeth and she was momentarily distracted by the clear blue of his eyes. She took a breath to regulate her heart, which had inexplicably started beating harder.

"I have heard already some of what occurred," Gabriel admitted. "When I arrived in the fields this morning there was much chatter and gossip. Most of it stopped as I approached but I heard enough."

"So you know that my mother, Lady Mary, has married again and to whom she is now pledged?"

"Yes, I do." His answer was brief yet his tone spoke much more.

"My brother has reminded Master de Ath of the rights that Rogier and I hold regarding the manor."

"You know, my lady —"

"Elizabeth," she interrupted.

He grinned. "You know, Elizabeth, that you and Sir Rogier have my complete loyalty. I shall of course inform you should there be anything of detriment to this manor … from any source."

As Elizabeth lifted the hem of her green linen dress and descended the stairs from her solar, she was thinking of her first task for the day, which was to speak with the cook about the meals for the week and take an inventory of the spice cupboard. A trip to the market at Stamford and haggling over prices was the last thing she wanted to do right now, and she hoped there was sufficient to last until the following week. There was too much to do to go traipsing across the countryside. Perhaps she could detail Mary to go. She may enjoy the outing, for she had been melancholic these last few day. This was surprising since she was newly married, although the noises Elizabeth had heard coming from the bedchamber had not been joyful.

As she drew near the screened-off corridor to the left of the fire, Elizabeth heard Bartholomew holding court with a few other men. She paused to listen.

"Yes, the Jacquerie in northern France is well within memory," one of the visitors said.

"What was that?" another asked.

"Oh, surely you know of that." She recognised Bartholomew's arrogant tone. "The peasants — the jacquerie in France. They called their leader Jacque Bonhomme but his real name was Guillaume Caillet. That uprising saw two months of bloody violence. We don't need to see similar in England."

"Indeed not. The serfs and villeins here all have those padded jackets, too."

"I have one," someone spoke up. "I have mail, too, which belonged to my uncle."

"Most of us have some sort of armour. It's only to be expected. You never know when we may have to fight," a different voice added.

"I know they had no real grounds against the nobility," continued Batholomew. "Froissart's *Chroniques*, of which I have had sight, told of unimaginable horrors — of murder and destruction — but the rightful order was restored when French nobles led by the Dauphin captured the ringleader. He was decapitated." There were general murmurs of appreciation. "I have the measure of the folk at this manor. Fear not, my friends, there'll be no uprising here."

"Didn't Denmark have trouble too?" someone asked.

"Oh yes, something to do with the region known as Estonia. Not for us to concern ourselves." Bartholomew was dismissive.

"There are mumblings across this region, you know," one of the men said. "The poorer serfs aren't happy with the increased workload and the wealthier ones think they should be paid more or have more land upon which to grow food."

"Oh, I know all about that," responded Bartholomew. "Don't forget I own many hectares to the east of here. I have a finger on that pulse, well enough. I have plans in hand. The villeins need to be certain who's in charge here."

Elizabeth was tempted to return to the hall and upbraid Bartholomew, but thought better of it. She wondered whether his 'plans' were real or if he was simply boasting to his companions. She hoped he had heeded Rogier's words. He was not in charge here.

Later that day, Elizabeth went out to the gardens to gather herbs for the evening meal. While this was not something she would normally do, being the preserve of the kitchen maids, she had craved some fresh air and the aroma of the herb beds beckoned. She had a pleasant time wandering between the herbs, breathing in their scents, both delicate and pungent, and taking solace from the birds' songs all around. As she left the walled area, she saw Marcus leaving the hall and crossing the inner bailey. Elizabeth was puzzled. What was he doing here? He should be overseeing the last of the harvest or supervising the threshing. It was a critical time of year for that. She was still puzzling about it as she entered the great hall and headed for the kitchens with her basket of herbs.

She heard the door to the parlour open on the far side of the fireplace and Master Bartholomew appeared.

"Master Bartholomew." She nodded an acknowledgement. "I'm surprised to see you using the parlour. It's usually reserved for conversations of a more private nature. Of business matters, even."

"Indeed. Perhaps someone wished to speak with me."

"Who might that have been?" She was being impolite but she cared not.

Bartholomew sighed. "As it happens the reeve wanted my advice."

"Your advice? I trust you referred him to my brother or to me, since you understood my brother's instruction, I hope?"

"You were not to be found," he said. "It was of little consequence."

"Nevertheless, I believe you should share it with me, since the manor is my responsibility in my brother's absence."

"It was a matter related to the ditches. Really nothing at all." His eyes slid away. "I told Master Reeve to speak with you, naturally." He picked at an imaginary mark on his sleeve, before returning his gaze to her. "I'm sure he will find you in due course." There was challenge in his eyes.

Elizabeth felt ill at ease and determined to go in search of Marcus as soon as she had been to the kitchens with her basket.

The heat of the ovens hit her with full force as she entered the kitchens, but it was the cook who took her attention. She was remonstrating with the butler while the two undercooks, the cupbearer and the spit boy watched on aghast.

"You've gone too far, this time, Master Clegg," Cook said, her face red and sweaty. "I think you better return to your buttery and sober up before dinner needs to be —" She caught sight of Elizabeth and halted her tirade.

"Mistresh!" The butler slurred his acknowledgement of her presence.

"Master Clegg, I will speak with you in the buttery. Please go and await me there." Elizabeth watched him stagger away in none too straight a line before she turned to Mistress Cook, who was still brandishing a ladle.

"How long has this been a problem?" she asked.

"Not long, m'lady. Only since he lost his Martha. That girl was the light of his eye and he was overjoyed when he heard he was going to be a grandfather again. Her death has hit him hard."

"I'll speak to him. Thank you."

As she headed to the buttery she was overcome with remorse. She should have realised the man was still mourning the loss of his daughter. While other members of the nobility tended to ignore the welfare of their workers to some extent, Clémence had taught her humanity and taught it well. Now she must follow her grandmother's lead.

Thus, all thoughts of Marcus and Bartholomew were put to the back of her mind, albeit temporarily.

CHAPTER 9

Mary appeared for dinner in the great hall after everyone was seated. Her eyes were downcast as she dropped a brief curtsey to the company before taking her seat next to her husband, whose brow creased in a frown. Bartholomew's friends were still with them and already the atmosphere was merry among the men, their laughter becoming raucous, so Mary and Elizabeth said little. One of the men tried some light banter with Isabelle, but her smile was thin and when she did not pursue the conversation, he turned his attention back to the men, who were regaling each other with deeds of daring when out on their last hunt.

Elizabeth noticed her mother's eyes alight on her husband, but discerned no joy there. Certainly the previous adoration had disappeared; in fact, Elizabeth might have believed she recognised dislike. Mary looked down at the food on her platter, pushing it around with her knife before stabbing a tiny piece of meat and slowly lifting it to eat. And so it continued until she stopped eating altogether and pushed her platter aside.

The meal finished, Mary took to her room. Isabelle, too, disappeared, though Elizabeth didn't know where. She herself did not want to stay in the presence of the men so decided to visit the orchard and sit under the trees with her embroidery ring. The bells for compline, which would chime from the abbey calling the monks to evening prayer, was still some time off. The sun had not yet disappeared behind the trees and although the heat had gone from the day, it was mild and peaceful. She took out her embroidery. Her skilful fingers were working on a scene depicting the harvest, although she was undecided whether to include the accident with the cart that had killed Martha and her child. It was a fact of farming life and not unusual, but she was loathe to depict something so tragic.

After a few moments, she became aware of Gabriel standing a little way off with his hand resting above him on the branch of an apple tree.

She grinned at him. "Have you been sent to spy on me, Master Smith?"

"Forgive me, my lady, but I did not wish to disturb you when you looked so content."

"And I shall not be content if you insist on referring to my title rather than my name," she replied with a laugh.

Elizabeth's laugh was like the brook bubbling over the pebbles, and Gabriel was enchanted all over again. In truth, he had been watching her, admiring the way the sunlight sparkled on the tendrils of hair that escaped her coif, the smooth complexion of her face, tanned and freckled from hours spent in the fields helping with the harvest, and now, when she looked at him, the soft brown of her eyes, which seemed infused with the soft green of the moss of the forest floor. She had grown into a beautiful woman and he had to resist the impulse to enfold her in his arms. Instead he advanced slowly, for he was loathe to burden her with his news.

Her position as daughter of the manor would forever be a barrier between them, his status being ao different to her own. She would marry a knight or a nobleman befitting her status and he … well, he didn't know.

"So, what is it for which you seek me out?" Elizabeth asked.

Gabriel took a deep breath. "It involves Sir Bartholomew and my brother. It seems they have discussed the recent restlessness, particularly those of lower standing who are the most dissatisfied." He didn't need to explain their dissatisfaction. Elizabeth was well aware of rumblings both locally and in the wider region regarding workload and pay. "It seems that Master Bartholomew is of the opinion that they should be worked harder so they have no energy or time for discontent. Marcus agrees."

"But you do not agree." She indicated for him to sit next to her.

Gabriel sat down on the grass, aware of their proximity. "Indeed, I do not."

"Batholomew said they had talked about the ditches, but he made light of it," Elizabeth said. "I was suspicious there was more to it. Rogier warned him not to involve himself in manor business."

"Marcus is going to instruct the workers that all ditches must be cleared before they hold any harvest celebrations."

"There are many furlongs of ditches, especially at the eastern side of the estate's land where the ground falls away to the Fens," Elizabeth said.

"That's true. It will take several weeks of hard labour and Michaelmas is almost upon us. They will all expect the usual harvest supper and festivities. It's one of the times they look forward to most and…"

"And it is our thank you to them for all their labours when we give food and ale to each. If we make an enemy of our own people we will all suffer."

"Marcus had better be careful for himself, too, for as you know Michaelmas is his hiring day," Gabriel said.

"That is true, but I could no more tell him his work is finished here as suspend the festivities."

"Would you like me to speak to him?"

Elizabeth frowned in thought before answering. "No, I should do that. In many ways he is a good reeve, but I must make him see sense. Thank you for bringing me this information."

Gabriel got to his feet. "I shall leave you now." He paused. "I hear the bells of compline and it grows dark."

He breathed deeply and took in her perfume, reminding him of meadowsweet and the yellow roses that grew in the walled garden of the manor. His yearning to hold her close returned. He bowed to her and, desiring a touch however brief, he could not resist taking her fingers in his own and brushing a kiss over her hand.

Elizabeth watched Gabriel leave before standing. A strange feeling had come over her and she was still aware of his warmth of his lips as they had grazed the back of her hand. He was gallant and kind, brave and loyal. He owned all the qualities of a good knight, perhaps more so, in that he discussed aspects of higher learning with the monks at the abbey. But he was no knight. She gave a small moan before straightening and returning to the manor.

She spent most of the night thinking about how to approach Marcus, and finally decided to meet with him in the formal setting of the manor rather than speak to him in the fields. It was imperative to stamp her authority as lady of the manor. However, she was also aware that she must not make an adversary of the reeve. She must temper her rule with praise for the work he was doing generally. How she wished Rogier was with her, but she determined to do this and do it with sensitivity.

When Marcus knocked on the parlour door, Elizabeth indicated for him to take a seat at the table. He looked nervous. He wouldn't look her in the eye and fidgeted in his chair.

"Master Reeve, I wished to speak with you to clarify one or two things. You are not in trouble."

He looked at her then, but fleetingly.

"It's important to be clear that you take your instruction from me when my brother Sir Rogier is not here. Before he died, Sir Ruadhán made Sir Rogier and I guardians of my mother and as a result we hold the reins for matters regarding all aspects of the manor. No one else."

Elizabeth saw a look of challenge in Marcus's eyes as he glanced up at her.

"Perhaps this was not made clear and perhaps that is my fault." She saw his shoulders drop slightly and released a breathe she did not realise she had been holding. "Did Master Bartholomew suggest differently, Master Reeve? For if he did, I understand why you thought you should agree with him."

Marcus shrugged. "Maybe, my lady."

Having given him an escape route for his scheming with her stepfather, Elizabeth continued, "Well, it is clear now, so let us discuss what needs doing, that is the ditch-clearing, the workload for the serfs, and the celebrations for Michaelmas."

She proceeded to outline the schedule of work over the next few weeks, ensuring that the festivities were included. The weekend of celebrations was set and some of the details of provisions given by the manor outlined.

"Is there anything you wish to ask me, Master Reeve?"

"No, my lady." Marcus pushed his chair back prior to leaving the table.

"Just one more thing before you go. Your position as reeve is critical to the smooth running of the manor. I hope you will be happy to continue when we review things at Michaelmas. You are efficient and you know the workers. You are an asset to us in this role."

For the first time there was a small smile. "Thank you, my lady. Will that be all?"

"Yes, please implement the plans I have outlined."

As he left the room Elizabeth heard a commotion at the main entrance. She entered the hall to see Rogier striding towards her. "Sister, I have a day's leave of absence to ensure all is well here. I see you have been conferring with Master Reeve."

"Come, let's talk in the parlour, where we may be private in our discourse. I shall send for refreshments."

Once wine and biscuits were brought and the door firmly closed, Elizabeth shared the latest events with her brother. Rogier agreed with her decisions and she was unsurprised at his reaction to Bartholomew's interference. Fortunately, he was tired and unwilling to pursue the incident with their stepfather straight away. Perhaps in time he would let it pass, but Elizabeth had already determined to speak with him later, to reinforce what Rogier had told him previously.

At dinner that evening none of Sir Bartholomew's crowd were there. They must have had word that Rogier was home and decided absence was the greater valour on this occasion. Rogier allowed Mary to sit at the head of the table in front of the salt, in deference to her position, which pleased her greatly. Bartholomew sat on her right hand so he might share her cup and Rogier on her left. Isabelle sat next to her father and Elizabeth next to her brother. Thus, they were an intimate gathering, with most formality abandoned, and although they were not affiliated in many ways, the tension was muted.

Isabelle's delicate features were accentuated by the flickering candles that lit the table and Elizabeth was aware of Rogier's glances in her direction. She was content with her brother's distraction, since his interest in the young woman ensured his mind was elsewhere rather than upbraiding Bartholomew.

The meal progressed with everyone assuming good etiquette, wiping their fingers on the small towels provide, holding the stems of the cups to avoid sticky fingerprints, and Elizabeth noticed that her stepfather ensured Mary had the choicest pieces of meat from their shared trencher. He was obviously on his best behaviour. Perhaps Rogier's previous remonstrance had had some effect, though Elizabeth trusted him not.

Elizabeth watched Mary covertly. She rarely looked at her husband and when she did, she did not smile. At one point she dropped a knife among the rushes and flinched when Bartholomew raised his arm to summon a serf to retrieve it and wipe it clean. Something was very wrong.

Later that night Elizabeth discovered what that might be and she was shocked. As she drifted off to sleep, sounds from her mother's chamber crept into her consciousness. Sounds she tried to ignore, but then words penetrated the wooden walls.

"Remove thy shift, Wife."

Oh no. Elizabeth buried her head beneath the covers but after several moments she thought she would suffocate. She climbed from her bed and went to the window to breathe in the scents of the night and calm her racing heart. But she could not escape the voices next door.

"Kneel before me."

"What?" Mary's voice was high-pitched.

"You may pray while I divest myself of my attire. Closer. You cannot reach me from there, woman."

Elizabeth heard her mother whimper followed by a deep male groan before she placed her hands over her ears.

She thought she heard a cry and she removed her hands ready to race next door, but then all was silent. She returned to her bed and lay awake for a long time. She was unaware of when she fell asleep, but when she awoke it was daylight and she hurried with her morning preparations before descending to the hall to break her fast.

Mary was already seated at the table, her head turned away as Elizabeth approached. Of Sir Bartholomew there was no sign.

Elizabeth muttered a blessing for this before she greeted Mary. "Good day, Mother."

"Daughter, blessed is the day." Mary mumbled her greeting.

Elizabeth reached for bread before drinking from her cup of ale. As the servant, Avice, served them, the silence stretched out between mother and daughter. Elizabeth liked Avice, she was a pretty girl whose father was a senior sokeman. But Elizabeth needed to speak with Mary alone and dismissed the servant. "Mother, is all well with you? Only you seem —"

Mary turned her head and Elizabeth gasped. Her lip was cut and upon her cheek a bloom of blue that could be mistaken for nothing else but a bruise forming.

"What has happened?"

"It's nothing and you will say naught, do you hear me?"

Elizabeth left her seat and placed her arms around Mary's shoulders. Her mother's voice came as a whisper. "I made him cross. 'Twas not his fault. It will not happen again. I know now what I have to do. It will not be repeated," she said, as if willing herself to believe it. "Please do not speak of it — to anyone. What goes on between a man and his wife is for no one else to interfere."

If she may not speak of it, Elizabeth determined to watch with care. She understood that a man may do whatever he wished with his wife. She was his property. However, Clémence had taught her that life could be joyful with the right man and Ruadhán would never have treated her grandmother thus. Holding Mary close, Elizabeth resolved never to wed, should any man be likely to treat her thus, although she knew in her heart that things were not so straightforward for someone in her position. A lady she might be, but it was still her lord's wishes that could prevail, and Lord John in his castle at Folkingham had the right to say who she would marry. If it could gain him more land, and therefore power, he could choose anyone for her.

CHAPTER 10

The severe famine at the beginning of the century, caused by years of wet weather causing the crops to rot where they grew, followed by the Great Mortality when half the population had died, was still taking its toll. The unusual steps that Clémence and Ruadhán had the foresight to take to keep their people safe through those dreadful years had saved many, but not all would listen and several families had refused to come to the manor during those times and had struggled on. In the end, many had succumbed. Elizabeth understood the current dissatisfaction. With the depleted population and too much work with smaller rewards, they saw little worth in their future.

As the family and some of the higher ranking free sokemen gathered around the fire in the great hall one evening, the conversation inevitably turned to the topic that was on everyone's lips.

"The serfs understood the taxes that the Church raised back then and before the first poll tax. It seemed fair that it was a percentage of their counted goods. They may have hidden some when the church commissioner came round, but in all, they paid and did not resent it." It was Gabriel who spoke.

"Yes, as a fractional tax, and even when the government took over the process to finance this wretched, never-ending war with France, people accepted it."

"The second poll tax was far too complex," said Master Pullen, shaking his head, "with thirty-three bands. Ridiculous! Many began to resent things eighteen months ago when it was introduced."

"Have a care, Master Pullen," Master Oates said. "None of us like what's happening but Lord John of Gaunt, our Duke of Lancaster and the king's uncle, still holds the power and if he gets wind of such talk, well... Our own Lord John at Folkingham is his man through and through. Be careful what you say around here."

"The poll tax requires everyone over the age of fifteen to pay one groat — I heard that the poorest families are hiding their youngsters away when the government commissioner comes round to collect his monies," said Master Miller.

"The last revenue didn't yield anything like as much as the king and his uncles expected," Master Pullen added.

"If I learned who didn't pay, then they would be reported straight away," declared Sir Bartholomew haughtily. "That's robbery and no less."

"But Master de Ath, it's almost impossible for some to pay that amount. It's a day's labour simply to pay the commissioner, when they hardly have enough to eat as it is."

"Everyone has to pay. Even Lord John at the castle, and he must be on the top rate. That's six pounds, thirteen shillings and four pence." Bartholomew nodded with importance that he knew such things. "We landowners have to pay in pounds not pence. The serfs should think themselves lucky that we look after them as well as we do. A groat — four pence — pah! That's nothing."

The three sokemen glanced at each other. Elizabeth could tell from their worried expressions what they were thinking regarding her stepfather. She was unsurprised at Sir Bartholomew's intransigence, but could he not appreciate that his well-being was so closely tied to those of each worker? Her own thoughts turned to the poorest folk in the community. As was her habit, their food would be supplemented by her visit next week in time for the Christ's Mass.

She said nothing but her embroidery lay on her lap as she watched and listened. Mary continued with her sewing, showing no interest in the talk of the men. Elizabeth worried about her. There had been no further signs of brutality, but her mother had become distant and rarely smiled. Elizabeth knew not what went on behind the closed door of the marital chamber, nor did she wish to, but she still had responsibility for Mary's wellbeing, if her grandfather's wishes were to be fulfilled.

"I was at the monastery the other day," Gabriel said.

Elizabeth's attention was drawn back to the conversation.

"Father Prior told me of a class of people in Florence called the *Ciompi* — unrepresented labourers who do not belong to any guild but work in the wool trade. The city has seen three years of rioting and terrible bloodshed resulting from unequal taxation, unemployment and suffering. We don't want the same situation here."

"That's completely different, Brother," said Marcus. "The two situations do not equate at all." Elizabeth saw Bartholomew nod his head sagely, although she doubted he had ever heard of the *Ciompi*. As far as she knew, he had no interest in learning and never visited the monastery library or spoke with the more learned brethren there. Unlike Gabriel, she thought to herself, who spent his spare time searching out knowledge like a ferret after a rabbit.

"I'm simply saying that we should be careful what we demand of our workers here," Gabriel pointed out. "Perhaps we should listen so we might better understand their point of view."

"Surely you jest, sir," Bartholomew scoffed.

Elizabeth heard Gabriel sigh and saw Master Pullen raising a brow.

Just then Isabelle joined them from the shadows at the other end of the great hall.

"Ah, Sister," said Elizabeth, determined to be charitable towards the young woman. After all, it was not her fault her father was so offensive and disagreeable. Isabelle bobbed a curtsey to the company before Elizabeth made room for her on the wooden settle so she might be seated on a comfortable cushion at her side. Mary nodded an acknowledgement before continuing her sewing with her head down.

Isabelle must be lonely, Elizabeth thought, *and I have done nought to make her welcome*. Guilt encouraged her to ask, "Have you had a pleasant day?"

"I have been in my chamber, sewing for the most part."

"Perhaps tomorrow, if it continues fair, we might stroll together."

Isabelle gave a timid smile. "That would be most pleasant."

Before she could say more, Elizabeth's attention was taken with the latest news from the group of men.

"There is even talk of a new third poll tax, though nothing has been said officially. The monastery always has knowledge of court business," said Gabriel.

"It'll probably never happen, then, if it's simply talk," Marcus said. "Nothing to plague us."

"An unfortunate phrase, Brother."

"My apologies. So what is the rumour?"

"Father Prior suggested there might be a flat rate for everyone over the age of sixteen, but a greater sum than is currently collected. Anything up to thrice the current amount."

There was a murmur of disquiet. How could every man, woman, boy and girl afford that much when they couldn't pay the current amount?

"The king will have his coffers filled for his war in France somehow," Marcus said. "If that is what is decreed, then we must do our best to be good subjects and do his will."

"Marcus, you must see that this will break some people," Gabriel said.

Marcus shrugged. "It's just speculation and nothing for us to worry about."

Elizabeth frowned. She could foresee trouble if this new poll tax were to be implemented.

All conversation came to a halt as a sudden gust of chilly air entered the hall, lifting some of the rushes upon the floor. Two men advanced into the glow of the fire.

Isabelle leaped up and Elizabeth observed a sparkle in her eyes as they alighted on the visitors. But which one?

"Rogier! Sir Alaric! Welcome home, Brother, and good sir." Elizabeth placed her sewing down on the bench, bobbed a curtsey and went to her brother, offering both hands, which he took before kissing each. As she turned to Sir Alaric, he took the fingers of her right hand and raised them to his lips. His breath was warm against her skin and she smiled at the top of his blond head. Then he stood upright and inclined his head to the company before bowing fully before Mary. "My lady, such a pleasure to see you again."

"How pleased we are to see you, Sir Alaric, and my son." Mary turned to Rogier and said, "It has been a while but you are most welcome. I look forward to hearing how you are doing at the castle."

There was a some bustling as a request for refreshments was issued.

"Ah, a good lamb's wool will be just what we need," Rogier said with hearty joviality. "Don't you agree my friend?"

"Indeed," replied Sir Alaric. "Warm ale and brandy is what's needed on such a frosty night."

The servants rushed towards the kitchen to do the bidding and bring the drinks.

"And be certain the apples are well fluffed on the top," Rogier called after them. "The ale needs to be warm enough to make them pop open fully." He turned to the company. "It will soon be Christmas, and Lady Katherine bade us visit. Lord John will arrive at the castle soon and then it will be difficult to get away."

"Have you been busy at the castle?" Elizabeth the two young men. Sir Alaric had already received his dubbing, being slightly older than Rogier. His shoulders were broad and he carried an air of importance with his height and confident gaze.

"Indeed, we have," Rogier replied. "We have planned a grand *tournée* for the turn of the next season. It will celebrate the birth of Lord John and Lady Katherine's son, Lord Henry. The invitations will be issued shortly."

"That will be something to look forward to, will it not, Mother?" Elizabeth addressed Mary in a cheerful tone. "Perhaps you will have a new dress. Don't you agree, Sir Bartholomew, that for such an occasion new clothing is called for?"

"Certainly. We have a position to maintain and in the presence of Lord and Lady Beaumont we must demonstrate that we are people of importance."

"And your plans?" Rogier asked Elizabeth, though his gaze rested upon Isabelle, whose complexion turned prettily pink.

"We will be visiting the village and taking baskets of gifts to the poorest serfs. Will you gentlemen accompany us? Perhaps you, also, Master Bailiff?"

Gabriel nodded his assent.

"We shall be a merry company and hopefully bring some cheer to those who need it," Alaric said.

"Mother, will you be joining us?" Rogier asked, and Elizabeth eagerly awaited her answer.

"I think not," Mary said, looking at Sir Bartholomew. "I have tasks here to complete."

"Surely they can wait," said Elizabeth. "The fresh air will do you good."

"You heard your mother," said Bartholomew. "She will remain here, with me."

The next day a heavy-duty cart with two large wheels, capable of traversing the rutted tracks, was brought to the door. Elizabeth and Isabelle donned warm woollen cloaks over their warmest clothes, for the winter weather had brought ice to the early morning. Serfs brought baskets from the kitchens to be loaded onto the cart. Within each basket was placed a chicken ready for the oven, some lard, a tart filled with cheese, and a jar of pickled fruits and small onions soaked in verjuice, from the last of the unripe grapes. There was also some fruits stewed in honey, and a loaf made from maslin wrapped in a cloth. This mixture of rye and wheat, grown in one field as insurance against the failure of the wheat should the season be wet, was not as fine as pure wheat bread, but would still be a treat compared to the hard brown bread the poor were used to soaking in ale before eating. Finally, there was a screw of rough paper containing a small amount of valuable salt, and a radish, to be eaten with a small flagon of cider vinegar in the event of belly bloat. This was a common occurrence for those who were unused to rich food.

They were a merry company. The ladies sat on blankets in the back of the cart with Sir Alaric to keep them amused, while Rogier took the reins of the horse. Elizabeth could see from the grin on his face as they set off that he was enjoying the opportunity to show off, probably because Isabelle was gazing up at him with her large grey eyes. Gabriel walked beside the horse, with its head on the left, as was the custom.

The first cottage they reached was a single-roomed dwelling. It had good cedar shingles on the roof, for which the manor paid, since Ruadhán had ordered that no thatch was to be used where rats could live and breed following the Great Mortality. Thus, the smoke from the hearth rose through a hole in the roof rather than seeping through the thatch as in days past. Inside, the floor was covered in rushes, and the only light came from two tiny windows. Elizabeth deposited her basket on the plank table before which a man sat, his wife standing beside him, a baby on her hip. The air was filled with the odour of damp earth and the peat fire, but it was reasonably warm and a dog lay on the earth floor, chewing on something. Elizabeth could smell the dung of a cow that resided under the same roof during winter, for the shared warmth.

"Oh, my lady," said the goodwife. "You are right good to us. Many Christmas blessings to you."

There was a shuffling at the door and Gabriel came in. Of Isabelle there was no sign.

"Hello, Joseph, Mary-Anne. How is little William? He looks hale and in good spirits."

"Oh yes, Master Bailiff. He fares well. And grows fast. Thank you, sir, for asking. We are blessed that the good Lord has seen to spare this one from illness thus far." The goodwife made the sign of the cross. "We are doubly blessed to have a boy."

"He will help and relieve you of much as he grows older," Gabriel said.

Elizabeth could hear genuine interest in Gabriel's voice, and understood why he was so well-liked by the workers. There was no falseness about his words.

Having bestowed and received good seasonal wishes Gabriel escorted Elizabeth outside, where Alaric and Rogier waited. Isabelle stood with them, looking cold. Rogier helped Isabelle back into the cart, which brought a wan smile to her face, while Alaric took Elizabeth's elbow to do the same.

Gabriel forced a smile as he took his place by the horse's head, ready to march to the next humble house. His glanced back furtively as the young knight helped Elizabeth into the cart, his ears straining to catch the light-hearted exchange of conversation between them. As children, he and Elizabeth had played together as friends; now that they were adults, Gabriel realised he wanted so much more. But that was impossible. Although his father had been a senior sokeman before his passing, and Gabriel was now bailiff to the manor house, his position was still lowly compared to that of Lady Elizabeth Amundeville d'Albert.

He was intelligent, learned, he could be courtly, but still … he was lowborn.

As he mused, he thought of Elizabeth's grandmother Clémence, who had been the daughter of a mason but risen to become lady of the manor. But that was different, he thought morosely. Lord Ruadhán had chosen her.

Mentally shaking himself from his sullen thoughts he looked around. He had much for which to be thankful. Praise God he was healthy, had a profitable position, food and warm clothing. These people they were visiting had little compared with him.

Yet, when he looked at Elizabeth with her beautiful eyes and gentle intelligence, he desired her above all others.

CHAPTER 11

Christmas came and passed with the usual round of feasting, mummers, foolery and fun. At last, the weather turned warmer and the rain lessened. There was always the worry that the early season would be too wet for the crops to take. Memories of great puddles in the fields, rotting the tender roots and vulnerable shoots, still lived in peoples' minds. Those years had resulted in famine and death for many.

Now, the trees were sprouting their finery. The copper green of the oaks' newest shoots contrasted with the pure and vibrant birch. The willows along the river near the church were gilded with yellow as their sweeping sprays brushed the water as it bubbled over the stones, and leaves burst forth.

Excitement for the *tournée* at the castle was mounting, too, with talk of little else. The women planned their outfits in an array of polychromatic colour so different to their everyday dresses. There was a range of fabric; from heavy and starched, ensuring the wearer walked with serenity, to that which fell in gentle and flattering folds of delicate sheen. The ladies at the manor had paid several visits to Stamford, and had even sent to Lincoln and Burgh St Peter for a wider selection of ribbons and lace from which to choose to trim their garments. Hair coverings had caused much discussion and deliberation. Coifs and linen wimples were replaced with softer fabrics. Mary favoured the *kruseler* with its rows of gathered frills framing her face and a scarf which covered her neck and shoulders. It was a design which Anne of Bohemia had brought from her native lands and who was, at last, announced betrothed to King Richard himself. Complicated negotiations for the marriage had recently been completed, and her fashions were becoming popular among the nobility. Seamstresses worked all the hours of daylight and even by candlelight into the night to have the outfits ready.

The local men polished their weaponry. In line with the Statute of Arms for Tournaments, swords and axes were blunted to help curtail the bloodshed at tournaments. Although it was an ancient rule to which they must all adhere, there would still be injuries. There was great exhilaration for the events, which would include the mêlée, hand-to-hand combat and jousting. Long gone were the days when the tournament might be used as a subterfuge for an assassination. Now it was all about courtly romance and pageantry, when knights would pay homage to a lady of their choosing.

The mêlée was a mock battle held on the last day of the tournament. Two opposing teams, either on foot or horse, smashed into each other, with the aim of throwing the other team back or breaking their ranks. The last King, Edward numbered three, encouraged during his reign and so it continued. It created much nervous excitement among participants and spectators alike. This is when most casualties would originate, but the skills of warfare were sharpened and the participants anticipated the glory of demonstrating their prowess to those watching. Several fields were earmarked for the mêlée and the two teams would continue all day and even into the next if there was no satisfactory conclusion.

Many knights travelled from afar for the prize money on offer, for a tournament could be very profitable for such skilled fighters.

The domestic servants at the manor were in a flurry of activity to provide food and accommodation, either in the manor itself as a vassal of Folkingham Castle, or in tents set up on the estate grounds. Stands were erected outside the castle walls for spectators, with those who were residents on one side and onlookers from elsewhere on the other.

Good wine and food aplenty would be provided by Lord Beaumont at the grand party held in the evening of the first day, and there would be play-acting and storytelling involving mythology and acts of courtly love.

There was, however, one area of discord which was causing much debate and strife for the young men organising the event, including Rogier. King Richard had requested that Lord John, as a privy councillor and therefore his representative, should issue a livery badge with its white hart embroidery to all the local knights and squires. It had only been only four years since someone boasting John of Gaunt's badge, the king's unpopular uncle, had been pulled from his horse and the badge ripped away. Such was the high feeling for emblems when worn by private armies of retainers used to enforce a lord's will through baronial bullying.

Fortunately, at the last minute, King Richard changed his mind, having realised that the livery badges were becoming a protracted controversy of his reign and a delicate situation was resolved, much to everyone's relief.

The grand party was a remarkable sight. "I cannot imagine how much all this must cost," Elizabeth whispered to Rogier, who was merry with wine and pleased with how the first day of the *tournée* had gone.

"At least forty pounds, Sister."

"Forty pounds? That's outrageous! I could pay our blacksmith for five years with that amount of money."

"Hush, Elizabeth. That's a drop in the ocean for Sir John and don't forget he celebrates the birth of a son. His line will continue."

Elizabeth looked around for Lady Katherine. She sat on a dais watching the festivities, but looked pale and tired. Perhaps she was still not recovered from the birth of the child. As she watched, she noticed Sir Bartholomew talking to Lord John and was instantly concerned. He was taking a risk approaching their host at such a gathering as this. What on earth could their conversation be about? She moved closer through the throng the better to hear their words.

"She is certainly of an age to wed, sir," said Sir Bartholomew. "We should be most grateful, my lord, if you would give it your consideration."

"Yes, yes." Lord John took a long quaff from his goblet and Elizabeth could see his eyes roving elsewhere.

"Perhaps you might consider Sir Egbert of Heydour? Since his last two wives departed this life —" Bartholomew made the sign of the cross — "I believe he may be looking for a younger wife this time? Elizabeth is young and fertile and her grandfather and indeed her father were loyal to this estate, my lord." He bowed his head obsequiously.

"Leave the matter with me, sir..." Lord John hesitated, as if unsure of the man's name. "Confound it, where is my wife? Excuse me, sir."

Elizabeth was beside herself with anger. She had no wish to be married and certainly not to someone she barely knew and was old enough to replace her father.

"Why did you disappear so fast, Sister?" Rogier interrupted her thoughts.

Elizabeth took her brother's arm. "He's scheming to marry me off," she whispered in his ear, her voice hoarse.

"Who?"

"Bartholomew. He's been talking with Lord John and suggested I might be a good wife for that ancient who lives near Heydour!"

"Oh Elizabeth. Marriage will be inevitable before long. You cannot stay at Grimsthorpe forever. You must have heard of that new term, spinster — an unmarried woman who spends her time spinning — that's what you'll become if you don't marry." Rogier chuckled.

Elizabeth laughed too. "If I am to be a spinster, then I shall spin myself some bright yarn for colourful clothing. I shall sing and be lively, even when I am sixty years, God willing."

At that moment there was the sound of a gong and Lord John's seneschal announced the next entertainment. "Please make space for the *carola*."

Rogier took Elizabeth's arm and said, "Fear not, Sister. I shall speak with Katherine as soon as I may. She will be sympathetic to your plight."

At that moment, the children and young women of the entertainment entered to the accompaniment of pipes and soft drums. They were in a chain, their feet moving in rhythmic unison to the *estampie* steps, before forming their circle and joining hands for the singing of the sweet choral. There was no more talk between them.

Gabriel had heard all the details of the conversation between Lord John and Bartholomew regarding marriage for Elizabeth. Word always spread in a small community and he had many friends both around the manor and at the castle. He was greatly concerned for her. He had always known she would be expected to take a husband from her own class, or even a rank above, but the thought of her being shackled to one such as Sir

Egbert was too much and he debated for many hours whether he should speak to Rogier about it. Elizabeth herself would have little say in the matter. Such was the position of women, even one as independent as she. Though it hurt to know that she would never be his, he couldn't bear the thought of her submitting to that elderly glutton.

In the meantime, he dreaded meeting with her to discuss the manor's needs. Being enclosed in the parlour, so close to her, breathing her perfume, watching her expressive eyes, the curves of her body ... it was too much and best he avoided her.

It was several days before Rogier reported back to Elizabeth regarding the matter of her nuptials. He rode over one afternoon.

"I can stay but for a short while," he said. "Lord John is to depart on the morrow for London, though I shall not go with him, more's the pity. I am to help prepare his baggage train."

"Is Lady Katherine and the baby Henry to accompany him?" asked Elizabeth.

"No, she is with child again."

"So soon?"

Elizabeth pondered on Rogier's relationship with the young noblewoman. "I trust you are respectful of her, Brother. We do not need any scandal in that department."

"We are friends and no more. She loves her husband, Elizabeth."

"That's a relief. I wondered. You seem so familiar with her."

"We are friends of a similar age, and she is often alone."

"Exactly."

"There is no more to it than that. Rest easy, Sister. In fact, I was going to ask you something but, before that, I would tell you of my discussions with Lady Katherine regarding your future."

"I shall not marry Sir Egbert. I would rather throw myself off a cliff."

"Now you're being dramatic," Rogier said. "And where would you find a cliff in the Fens?"

Elizabeth had to bend to the will of her younger sibling because he was a man. It irked her and she tutted.

"I know, I know," he said, showing the flat palm of his hand to her. " Calm yourself. You have your own mind and I respect that, unlike our dear stepfather. He will do anything to further his own position and if that means he will make covert alliances to further himself through a marriage for you, he will."

Elizabeth had the grace to laugh and Rogier joined in her mirth.

"I have spoken with Katherine. She has influence with her husband in matters such as this. Frankly, he is not interested in the marriage of one of the lady's on his estates. He has more important matters of state to arrange. He will be visiting the king when he returns to London and they have many issues to discuss. There are murmurings of revolt by the lower classes, for one. I wish I could accompany Lord John to court —"

"Yes, yes," Elizabeth interrupted. "Please, tell me the nature of what Lady Katherine said to you."

"She is sympathetic. She married an older man, of course, but said she could not draw a comparison between Lord John and Sir Egbert. I am certain she will fight your cause and find someone more suitable."

"I'm relieved to hear that." Elizabeth clasped her hands in her lap. "Will she let me have a say? Perhaps I might be permitted to review the possibilities."

"Together we shall do our best for you. Whatever happens, Bartholomew will not have the last word, of this you may be certain."

Elizabeth nodded, then recalled that Rogier wished to ask her something. "So, what is your question of me?"

Rogier paused then glanced over his shoulder. She saw frown lines appear on his brow when he swept his hair away. *Why is he so ill at ease*, she wondered? "Come brother, it's not like you to be so reticent. What troubles you?"

Happy that no one else was near, he spoke at last. "It's our stepsister."

"Isabelle? What about her? She never causes any trouble. In fact, the reverse. She is so quiet and unassuming I hardly know she is here."

"But you do not dislike her?"

It was Elizabeth's turn to frown. "Where is this leading?"

"I think her a pippin," he said awkwardly.

"A pippin! You think her unique and highly admirable?" All was becoming clear to Elizabeth, but she managed to withhold her smile.

"Have you spoken to her of this?"

"No, nor would I wish to anger Sir Bartholomew. How best to proceed is my dilemma."

"Has she given you cause to think she may appreciate your company?" Elizabeth asked.

"I like the expression in her eyes when she looks at me. Her gaze softens."

"I suggest you find the time to walk out in the evenings and talk to her. Get to know each other better. You are away at the castle so much of the time. I shouldn't be counselling you on this. You should talk to someone like Sir Alaric."

"Ah yes, Alaric."

Elizabeth wondered at his enigmatic tone but instead asked, "Do you know when you will be made a knight yet? Perhaps you could go to court with Lord John if your status were to be lifted further."

Rogier became excited. "I do believe it will be soon. I have worked to become proficient in all areas of knightly combat. Lord John even commented that I am able to use sword, battleaxe and dagger above one of my age, and my aim with the crossbow is good.

"You have a courtly manner, I notice."

"I've passed all the more menial activities and on many occasions Lord John has selected me to dress him in his armour and trusted me with its upkeep. Perhaps in another year and I shall be dubbed and go to court with him."

"Would that I could be a knight," Elizabeth murmured, "instead of being at the mercy of men in power."

"In Catalonia there is the Order of The Hatchet. That's a military order for women to be in the knighthood." Rogier smiled at her.

Elizabeth sighed. "That's not my road, Brother. My life is here, as you know. I love the manor and our people."

"And you do very well by them, Sister. They are lucky to have you watching over them."

"Thank you. But there is a matter I must discuss with Master Reeve, regarding some non-payment by Master Pullen. He sees things in such a single-minded way. It makes him narrowminded when dealing with a concern."

"Do you wish me to stay and speak with him? I don't have long, though, as I must return to the castle."

"No, you must return to Lord John. I shall talk with Master Smith, but thank you, Brother. Return to your knightly duties and may Lord John see you are ready for your dubbing soon."

CHAPTER 12

It was another two days before Elizabeth finally managed to meet with Marcus. She summoned him to the parlour at the manor.

"Marcus, your position here is important to me," Elizabeth began. "As I've said before, you do your job well. However..." She took a deep breath and bolstered her reserve.

"My lady?" he sounded aggrieved and Elizabeth knew she must tread with care.

"It's this. Master Pullen is a sokeman and a steady worker. He has a standing among the village."

"Yes, and as such, with respect, my lady, he owes us honesty and loyalty. I could have him thrown off our land for his dishonesty."

Elizabeth sighed. "Tell me all."

"As you know, Master Pullen's sister left to marry and work on the estates in Surfleet. She went to help work the salt pans, where the River Glen goes into the wash."

"I am aware. But what is the grievance?"

"Well, you may not understand this, but he should have paid the merchet."

"I know what the merchet is. It's the fine paid upon marriage in recompense for the loss of a worker." Elizabeth controlled her irritation.

"He hasn't paid it."

"He must have his reasons. Have you spoken with him?"

"I have. He says his sister died from malaria as a result of the marshy ground out that way. He says he doesn't have to pay."

"But you don't believe him? You think he's lying about the death of his sister?"

Marcus nodded. "I do."

"What proof has he supplied?"

"A letter from someone he claims to be the local priest, but it's the wrong name. The man of God there is named Saul, not Thomas as on the bottom of the missive."

"Perhaps the man has changed. Have you enquired?"

"No, I have not seen the need." Marcus looked sullen.

"Before we proceed, send a messenger to Surfleet. Enquire who the current man of the church is. Do it straight away. We will get to the root of this matter one way or another. That will be all."

Marcus nodded, touched his forelock sullenly, and left the parlour. Elizabeth remained for several moments to regain her composure. How was it that two brothers with similar colouring and countenance could be so different? Marcus was a good reeve on the whole, she thought, but his short-sighted dealings with people were an irritation she could do without.

It was several days before Elizabeth asked Marcus the result of his messenger's mission to ascertain the whereabouts or otherwise of Goodwife Pullen.

"I still await an answer, my lady."

It was another two days before she discovered the reeve's duplicity. Marcus had consulted with Sir Bartholomew on the matter and as a result had not sent anyone to enquire at Surfleet. Instead, Master Pullen had been placed under house arrest. Elizabeth furiously paced her chamber, then decided to ride to the castle at Folkingham to find Rogier and discuss the matter with him.

She chose a mount for its speed and urged the stable lad to saddle it with haste. After commanding the young man to accompany her, they made good speed. Although still livid, the ride did her good. The rhythmic thundering of the animal's hooves, the wind in her face and the smells of countryside calmed her. It was less than an hour and they arrived with little lather for the horses and plenty of breath for herself.

At the gate she spied the same guard, Peter Parry, who had propositioned her before, and was pleased she had brought the stable lad along.

"Good day, mistress," he said, eyeing her legs as she dismounted.

"It is 'lady' to you," she said with disdain.

"And who shall I say is calling, *my lady*?" She wondered if he recognised her from the time previously when she had arrived late in the evening dressed in her brother's clothing.

"I am Lady Elizabeth Amundeville d'Albert of the manor at Grimsthorpe and I am here to see my brother, Sir Rogier, squire to Lord John and soon to be knight."

"I'll take your horse, *my lady*. They are all gathered in the great hall."

"I know my way."

Elizabeth dismissed him from her thoughts as she told her lad to feed and water the horses while she sought out her brother. As she entered the porch with its heavy door, she knocked and waited. It was opened by a servant seated just inside the door for this purpose. Elizabeth stated her business and was shown into the hall. Rogier stood with a group of other young men and women around a seated Lady Katherine. There was no sign of Lord John and she guessed he was away again at court. She dropped a formal curtsey.

"My lady," she said. "I hoped I might have a word with my brother. It is a family matter but one of importance."

"Certainly. It is good to see you again, Lady Elizabeth. Perhaps we might speak before you leave?"

"Indeed, my lady," Elizabeth said, bobbing another curtsey. She wondered what Lady Katherine might wish to discuss. She noticed Sir Alaric watching her as he listened to another, whispering an aside. She saw him grin and nod at what had been said, and then Rogier was by her side.

They moved together down the hall, away from the ears of the company, and Elizabeth explained the dilemma with regard to Bartholomew and the reeve. "So, you see, Master Reeve decided to discuss the issue of the non-payment with our stepfather, instead of sending to Surfleet as I commanded. I was quite clear about it. And now Master Pullen is under house arrest and there is talk of taking him to the prison cell in Burgh St Peter to await punishment."

Rogier frowned. "It should be for our own manor court to deal with. I shall send a messenger to Surfleet. As soon as we have the name of the current incumbent at the church who can verify the whereabouts of Goodwife Pullen, I shall send word to you."

"Thank you, Brother. Perhaps you need to speak with Marcus and Sir Bartholomew. Bartholomew has overstepped his position yet again, and Marcus resents my interference."

"I will speak with our stepfather. I laid the boundary for him before, as you know. I thought things had improved in that direction."

"They did, for a while. It seems he needs reminding."

"Sister, you should speak again with Marcus. He must see your authority. If this is not made clear, will never have sway with him and it may spread to others. Our grandfather was clear. You, in my absence, have the permission to run the manor and its estates. Enlist the support of Gabriel. He will support you and put his brother straight, surely."

"Indeed. I have no doubt of his skill and loyalty." Elizabeth's thoughts flashed to the bailiff and heat rose to her face as she pictured his strong physique and blue eyes. "I shall speak with him. Now, I believe Lady Katherine wishes to converse with me before I return to the manor — do you know what that is about?"

"I think you better see her and find out."

Elizabeth watched in admiration as Lady Katherine chatted easily with the group of young people who surrounded her. She guessed Lord John had taken all his more senior knights to court with him, for those who remained were all of an age with his young wife. As she watched, she understood better her brother's relationship with Katherine. She was young, attractive and vibrant. All were enamoured with her. When she referred to her husband, however, her expression softened. Clearly she missed his presence at her side. Rogier must have realised she was not for him and had looked elsewhere, hence his apparent attraction to Isabelle. Perhaps that was a passing infatuation. If he went to court, he would surely forget the wraith-like young woman who was so easily on hand.

When an opportunity landed, Elizabeth took a step forwards and said, "My lady, you wished for a word?"

"I hope you have completed your business with your brother to some satisfaction?"

"Yes, thank you, my lady." It was a polite answer, but the problem still remained until she spoke with Marcus and Rogier upbraided Master Bartholomew once more.

"Call me Katherine. We shall go to the parlour, where we may speak in private."

Someone leapt to accompany them with a light and, with disregard for the cost, lit the four fat beeswax candles which stood in a candelabrum on the table. There were no odorous tallow lights here, and the newly arrived variety that had come from Europe was definitely preferable. Elizabeth used them sparingly at the manor, for important guests, but at the castle they were everywhere. Now, they burned brightly in the small, intimate room. The parlour was similar to that at the manor but more sumptuously furnished, with rich hangings on the walls. No workaday rushes on the floor either. The stone flags were clean and a knotted rug of fine wool covered the area under the table and chairs, ensuring greater warmth for the toes. There was even a window with real glass, not the thin horn covering that many favoured as a cheaper alternative. Elizabeth thought she would prefer a clear view across the lawns rather than the distorted outlook seen through the expensive glass. Still, she couldn't blame Lord and Lady Beaumont for wanting to show off their great wealth and status.

Katherine indicated for her to take a seat and while she arranged her skirts in an oak chair at the head of the table, Elizabeth wondered if she would like a taste of this sumptuous living or even court life. The adventurer in her thought she might, but perhaps only a taste. There was too much strife, and a few people jostling for the highest honours could be the cause of a dangerous place, if all the talk of the king's uncles, especially John of Gaunt, were true. The relationship he had with his mistress, Katherine Swynford, caused upset when he granted her several estates, but this unease paled into insignificance as he raised a poll tax to fund increasingly unsuccessful campaigns in France. It was a vicious, regressive tax and the poorest people were hit hard. They heard of his lavish Savoy palace in London and that he owned vast tracts of land other than their own corner of England. Rumours began to circulate that he wanted his young nephew, King Richard's crown for himself as he seized more power.

Elizabeth sighed.

"Is all well with you, Elizabeth?"

She smiled. "Yes, my lady. All is well, thank you."

"I thought we might have discourse regarding your marriage," Katherine said.

Elizabeth's heart began to pound.

"I well understand how it is to be married to an older man. The name Sir Egbert of Heydour has been mentioned. We see such alliances all the time and it is usually for the benefit of someone other than the young bride." She smiled and Elizabeth noted gentle understanding.

"I really do not want to be wed to Sir Egbert, as my stepfather has suggested."

"I appreciate that, and times are changing, albeit only slightly. You have the right to refuse such a match."

"And I do, wholeheartedly!" Elizabeth spoke with intensity before adding with haste, "Forgive me, Katherine."

"I concur with your opinion. I could think of nothing worse should I be in your position. Fortunately, in my marriage, I have a love match and Lord John is only six years my senior. Rare, I know."

"I am pleased you are blessed with two sons, now. Is all well with you now? And the babe?"

"I was fortunate to make the pilgrimage to Walsingham where a vial of the blessed Virgin's milk is housed. That will have eased my passage. My birthing chamber was soothing and dark and the images on the walls were calming. I know I am fortunate, for many of our serfs and villeins do not have these aids. My husband bought me a gemstone girdle of amber and jasper which undoubtedly helped, too. I had poultices of eagle's dung and coriander. All this made a much easier time than I had for the first. This time, though, I'm not sure they burned the cord properly with little Henry. I do believe that all the sins that we committed at conception may have remained in him and that is why... Well, that is past now, and he will find his way in the world. He did sneeze well after birth; the herbs clearly did their work in exorcising the last few devils. I hope the vinegar on his tongue will bring speech in suitable time, though 'tis early days, of course."

"God be praised," Elizabeth said.

"So, to your situation. I have discussed it with my husband. He is content to let me talk with you. After, I shall speak with Master de Ath about my decision."

Elizabeth smiled. It seemed that in Katherine she might have an ally, although her heart's choice could never be. She thought of Gabriel and her heart quickened. In the end a marriage would be arranged for her and it would be based around the acquisition of lands.

"Elizabeth, the man I would choose for you would be Sir Alaric Swain. He is only your senior by a few years. I have seen the way he admires you. He is a favoured knight of my husband, though young still, and may well be at court very soon. You would have the opportunity to go with him."

Elizabeth blinked. "Thank you for your consideration, my lady." Both young women sat in silence for several moments as Elizabeth absorbed this proposal.

Finally, Katherine spoke again. "I am certain you will want time to consider my suggestion, but Sir Alaric is kind and fair of countenance." She winked and Elizabeth was aware that her cheeks were colouring. The thought of any form of intimacy with Sir Alaric was not so obnoxious as it was with Sir Egbert.

"I shall think upon your idea. I would dearly wish to remain in my home as much as possible. The manor was left to my brother and I to run by our grandfather, Sir Ruadhán Amundeville."

"I did not know him, having only come to live here since his passing, but he was an astute and brave man, I hear." She paused before adding, "This is Sir Alaric's home now. His older brother has his father's estates, but much of the time your husband will be away at court, or in France — the war still rages intermittently — or he will be working here at the castle. Between Rogier, yourself and your husband, you would be able to oversee the smooth working of the manor."

"Thank you, Katherine, for your understanding and sensitivity."

"As soon as you give me your decision, I shall inform your stepfather. I hope we will be friends, Elizabeth."

The young lady noted her new companion's choice of words. 'Inform' sounded good to her.

Elizabeth was quiet during the ride back to the manor. She had much to contemplate, foremost being the possibility of marriage. How would she manage to live with another man, who she did not love, when her whole being cried to be with Gabriel? But that was never to be and Alaric was personable enough. As Katherine had said, he would be away much of the time. In truth, she had little choice. It would be far preferable to other options and maybe she would even experience a soupçon of court life.

As they trotted over the wooden bridge, she was relieved to be home. The limestone walls of the manor were warm and inviting, safe and familiar. They enveloped the young woman, and contentment washed over her. All would be well, she thought.

CHAPTER 13

Elizabeth's wedding day dawned with a mist that was reluctant to disperse. The past few days had been glorious in their warmth and should have ensured her well-being, but she was in a stew of torment, unable to appreciate her surroundings in all their late spring glory. The grey dampness matched her mood.

There had been a flurry of correspondence over the last few weeks and Lady Katherine had lent her significant position to the negotiations. Eventually the dowry was agreed and though small, it was satisfactory, since Sir Alaric would be gaining more with this alliance than he had expected as the younger brother. He already considered himself fortunate not to be joining the priesthood. His family would see a rise in the esteem of others through this alliance with a family of ancestral renown.

Elizabeth, on the other hand, understood her fate could have been much worse, but she would rather not marry at all. Sir Bartholomew, in the end, had little power over the situation and he was well aware that the manor in which he lived would be gaining little and himself even less. His plans for further advancement through Elizabeth's marriage had been thwarted, and he was bad-tempered with all around him. Poor Mary received the greatest of his tongue lashings and as a result spent much time in her private solar, only emerging for meals.

When she saw Gabriel about the manor, she grieved. He was always courteous but she had the distinct impression he was avoiding her, and any camaraderie there had been between them was gone. He strode about looking more like his older brother than ever before. He was surly and frown lines creased his normally merry countenance. All joviality had vanished with the announcement of her impending nuptials and the grey morning of the day reflected not only her mood but his too.

Elizabeth had bathed and smoothed oil, sweet herbs and rose petals onto her skin before dressing in her best peacock-blue linen, coloured at vast expense. It was the shade of piety; of the Blessed Virgin. Pinned to her breast was the golden annular brooch she retrieved from the copper treasure box. At least Clémence would be with her in spirit and she would take courage from the thought. Isabelle had brushed her hair until it shone and she had then placed a simple veil over it, held in place with a circlet of flowers entwined with a fine gold wire.

A troop of minstrels had been employed to sound the passage of Elizabeth and her family to the church, as was the tradition. There was a bagpipe, a six-stringed viol, two flutes, drums, and a trumpet, and the music resounded around the small buildings of the village as they walked. A merry band of serfs, having been given time away from their labours, gathered behind them, the number growing as they progressed, so that by the time they arrived at the church there was over fifty people.

There was already a crowd awaiting them at the church as they arrived. Alaric was there, standing tall and looking proud, dressed in his finest attire. Elizabeth took her place at his left side as the Church demanded, woman having been fashioned from Adam's left rib.

The priest appeared from inside the church, and holding the *wed*, in this case a ring given by Alaric, he proceeded to ask the relevant questions as he held the gift aloft for all to see.

"How old are the bride and groom?"

"I am sixteen," Elizabeth said.

"I have twenty-three years, Father," Alaric announced.

"Are the bride and groom related to each other by blood?"

Sir Bartholomew answered. "They are not."

"Does the bride's father permit this marriage?"

"I do."

"Do the bride and groom consent freely to enter this marriage?"

Alaric answered promptly.

There was a pause and then Elizabeth gritted her teeth and made her reply. "I do."

The dowry agreement was read for all to hear, before the groom offered the bride a small purse with the required number of coins to give to the poor.

Alaric pledged his honour to her, to have and to hold her in bed and at table, to care for her whether she be fair or deformed, to care for her in sickness and in health and ending with "'Til death us depart," as required.

Elizabeth stood with her eyes lowered. Alaric would probably be kind, but with all her heart she wanted another and could tell neither of them her innermost thoughts. Her whole being rebelled and she was powerless to rectify any of this. Lady Katherine had decreed it, believing it was in Elizabeth's best interest; her stepfather had agreed to it, hoping to limit her presence; and her mother was so resigned to her own fate that Elizabeth could not confide in her.

Finally, the *wed* was blessed by the priest and passed to the bridegroom. Alaric took Elizabeth's right hand lightly in his own and after placing the ring on each finger in turn, he recited, "In the name of the Father, the Son, and the Holy Ghost, with this ring, I thee wed." Finally, he pushed it onto the fourth finger of her right hand. "The blood which flows directly from your heart to this finger seals our troth," he said, in time-honoured tradition.

It was done. Elizabeth's life was tied to this man and their future was sealed.

The priest proceeded to open the church doors so the bride and groom could follow him to the altar. After came their parents and other invited guests who stood in the nave to watch the canopy being held over the couple while Mass was performed. When all was done, they exited the building as a choir chanted the Agnus Dei. The familiar words, from nearly one thousand years before, calmed Elizabeth's soul so that the sun — which had burned through the mist while they were inside — seemed like a positive sign of things to come and enabled her to smile as she distributed the nuptial purse among the poor who had waited so patiently.

Gabriel waited with the rest of the senior members of the household for the party to return to the manor, even though the lack of activity caused anguish. He would have preferred to absent himself and start a physical task to detract from him torment.

"You seem tense, Brother," Marcus said as he stood at Gabriel's side.

Gabriel mumbled something about tasks awaiting before turning his head away and silently praying, *Please, dear Lord, I'll do whatever you ask so long as Elizabeth is light-hearted. Since she cannot be mine, let her be content with this young knight.*

As the family walked across the bridge, led by Elizabeth and Alaric, the waiting servants who lined the way to the door of the great hall threw flowers and clapped. Gabriel saw the woman he loved on the arm of another and his face grew tight. As they drew level, he saw Elizabeth's face and wondered at the tension in her smile before he lowered his own gaze in a nod of acknowledgement, so he would not have to lock eyes with her. After this brief respite, he lifted his head and gave a forced smile for the benefit of those around him. He attempted not to stare at Alaric's back with loathing for he knew the knight was known to be an honourable man who, while a touch arrogant, would probably be kind enough to his beloved. He was ashamed of his unjustified thoughts.

Gabriel must be careful. He did not want to be dismissed should a new order prevail at the manor. And now he must smile and be jovial at the wedding feast, although thankfully he would be seated a long way down the hall from the newly married couple.

On entering the great hall, Elizabeth noted the trestle tables set in two long rows, perpendicular to the one on the dais at which she and her new husband would be seated with their honoured guests. As the wedding party processed to their places all others took theirs, standing behind the benches placed along one side of each table. Thus, the serfs could easily fill plates and cups without reaching across anyone. Most guests had brought their own knife and drinking vessel, and there was a clattering as they were put down.

Rose petals were strewn among the rushes, and lilies stood in tall vases. The window linens were also open to the freshness of the afternoon and a gentle breeze graced the occasion, ensuring the scent of the flowers permeated the hall.

The bride and groom were placed at the centre of their table, despite some guests being of higher status. This was their day. Lady Katherine sat next to Alaric in deference to her rank, with his widowered father on her right side, since Lord John was still absent at court. Next to Elizabeth was Bartholomew, Mary and then Rogier. Each chair was graced with a cushion for they would be seated for several hours. Those on the benches must content themselves with wooden seats.

Now that the ceremony was over, Elizabeth relaxed a little, pushing what was to come later to the back of her mind. The food was ready, there was plenty to be had, and there were hours of feasting and entertainment before aught else.

There was roasted mallard, partridges and pheasants. In the centre of each table was a roasted boar's head with all the trimmings. There were stuffed chickens, pork pies and various flavours of rich pottage made with meat juices. Fish dishes came next with tench, and eels caught in the waterways of the Fens, as well as trout given with a blessing by the monks of Vaudey Abbey. Father Prior also sat at the top table, as a representative of the abbey, to enjoy all the richness and bounty of the wedding feast. He was a kindly old man and he was loved as a leader of the community. There was plenty of bread to soak up the thick spiced sauces. Another course was presented with wafers and cheeses, soft and mild, as well as almost crunchy with maturity. There were pies, tarts and pastries, sweetened with honey or wrapped around fruits, as well as candied peels. Accompanying each course was wine, as well as wine spiced or thickened with egg yolks.

Elizabeth managed to pick at each offering, sharing her platter with her new husband, who ate and drank with alacrity. She glanced at him and he caught her watching him and said, "Your family have given us wonderful fare. I trust you are as happy as I?" He grinned at her, and she saw he was cheerful and relaxed.

Elizabeth smiled at his enthusiasm but was saved from answering when Rogier called from his place, "Good cheer to you both, my sweet sister and my good friend." He raised his cup in salute before taking a gulp of his drink. Alaric raised his in return before finishing its contents in one long quaff then signalling for more.

Someone else shouted out, "Eat well and drink more, for you have a night's work ahead of you!"

This was followed by raucous laughter and some other forthright comments, which were fortunately curtailed by the arrival of two stilt walkers who led a small parade of assorted entertainers, including an acrobatic duo, one balanced upside down on the hands of the other. Both were dressed in garments of red and yellow, with painted faces. They were followed by jongleurs who came in singing and arranged themselves at the end of the hall facing the high table while others performed juggling tricks before they recommenced with a mixture of songs both bawdy and romantic.

At this point Father Prior stood and politely took his leave, meaning the party could proceed with unbound risqué fun.

Still more food arrived as the entertainment continued, but then it was time to usher the bride and groom to their nuptial bed. Alaric disappeared with several of his friends while Isabelle and other ladies ushered Elizabeth to a chamber where they helped her remove her wedding attire and don a fine linen shift.

There was much laughter and joking, fuelled by wine from earlier, and then all joined together in the marital bedchamber to witness the bedding. There was hardly space for everyone and there was much jostling before a monk from the abbey arrived to bless the couple.

Finally, the curtains around the bed were closed. Elizabeth heard shuffling feet as the crowd edged away, some dispersing back down to the hall to continue feasting, others falling back to the other side of the room to await what must be witnessed.

She was alone with Alaric for the first time ever and she was suddenly nervous.

"Don't be afraid," he said. "I shall not harm you."

Elizabeth was grateful for his perceptiveness.

"I don't know what to do," she whispered, and gave a nervous laugh.

"I do." He stroked her face and cupped her head, drawing her closer to him.

She smelled his masculine scent, the wine on his breath, and felt the warmth of his skin close to hers. Unbidden came the image of Gabriel's face, his azure eyes, his dark curls and his long-fingered hands. She gasped and Alaric mistook it for a sign.

Gently he undid the lace of her chemise. Guilt overtook her as Alaric's face rose above hers and she saw the desire there. She closed her eyes and tears crept down her cheeks to soak the linen-covered pillows beneath her head.

He was correct. He was kind to her and this first time didn't hurt much at all. She saw from his expression that he derived pleasure, and slept soundly afterwards, but Elizabeth lay awake for many hours.

Her silent prayers for forgiveness might go some way to alleviating the perjury of imagining she was with Gabriel, but she would need to seek absolution as soon as possible. Perhaps the priest would listen to her. Although he was an old man now, he had supported Ruadhán through some of his most testing times. Clémence always spoke highly of him. She'd loved him dearly and his wisdom must surely prevail. He would help her to understand and assume her new role with patience and perhaps eventually some alacrity.

The celebrations continued long into the next day and through to the evening, but eventually duties called and guests left to return to their own demesnes. Servants had much clearing to do and Alaric and Rogier had to return to the castle to continue their obligations.

CHAPTER 14

Only a brief time passed before Lord John called Alaric to London to be part of his retinue at court. Alaric had confided to Elizabeth that it was a mark of his lord's regard for him, and Elizabeth waited with anticipation to see whether he wished her to accompany him. She couldn't decide whether she wanted to be there or not. There were still undercurrents of unrest among the workers, which added to her indecision, and she was loathe to leave Mary. She was certain Bartholomew was over-heavy with her mother on occasions, for there was evidence of bruising and Mary was evasive when questioned. She could not come between husband and wife, but should she be away, perhaps Rogier could spend more time at home. Not yet dubbed a full knight, he would not be expected at court.

She loved the gentle pace of life at the manor and the familiarity of the lands upon which she walked with regularity. Even the days that were wet and inclement had a beauty in the vast skies that stretched forever as the land sloped away from the manor house over the dark Fen soil. The brightness of the leaves in the woods behind the village were turning a darker shade of green with the turning of the seasons, and on the forest floor the tiny bright celandines and wood anemones had been replaced by a carpet of bluebells. When she returned to the house she loved the way it wrapped its comfort around her

Alaric, like Rogier, would rather be about his knightly duties than supervising the manor, so much was left to Elizabeth. Bartholomew spent a deal of time out riding or hawking and she saw little of him, for which she was grateful. She decided to speak to Gabriel. He might have an opinion on whether her presence could be spared. She valued his thoughts and although they were still awkward together, he was always polite and eager to support her decision-making. Then she would talk to Rogier and point out that he could spend more time with Isabelle if he were to stay around his home more, should she be away.

She was certain Lady Katherine would agree with this plan. They had seen each other a few times since Elizabeth's wedding and found companionship, being of similar age and circumstance. Elizabeth had confided in her with regard to her stepfather and in turn, Katherine had told Elizabeth she was considering whether to ask Lord John if she might join him at court now the babe was settled. She told Elizabeth she missed the finery, the arts — of which King Richard II was so fond — and even the intrigue, having been away from court for a while. Her tales of life in London piqued Elizabeth's curiosity and if Katherine were there too, it would be so much more fun.

Elizabeth sought out Gabriel when she knew he would not be particularly busy and asked if he would walk with her in the manor grounds.

"Of course, my lady," he answered in response to her suggestion.

"My lady?" she said. "Why so formal all of a sudden?"

"You are married now and Sir Alaric is a knight. I am but a humble bailiff and do not wish to cause you awkwardness by being too forthright," then he added, "my lady."

His words troubled her. The blossom had all drifted away on the spring breezes and tiny apples were visible on the branches. Another year, another round of growth, ripening, and harvest to come. So the year turned, and Elizabeth normally took great comfort from it, but now…

Now her circumstances had changed. She was indeed married and when he was with her, Alaric expected the comforts to which a wife must submit. He was usually gentle, although sometimes his passion took hold and the act was over with speed. As she walked beside Gabriel and glanced up at his serious countenance, her whole being ached for things to be different. The social order must be maintained, but it was an agony when all she longed for was to be held by this man, kissed by him, touched… A shiver ran through her body.

Seeking distance in formality, Elizabeth cleared her throat and told Gabriel of her reason for meeting him. "I am expecting to accompany my husband to London before long. He has been called to court to be with Lord John."

"I see." Gabriel glanced away from her to where Avice, the servant girl, was cutting across the orchard towards the kitchen garden with a basket on her arm. "That will be a most interesting place to visit."

"Indeed, it will be. I do not relish leaving our manor, though. There is still a degree of unrest and while I anticipate Rogier being here more during my absence, I worry. My stepfather, as you know, is liable to take things into his own hands and that must not be."

"You speak frankly, my lady. Remember I am only the bailiff."

Elizabeth stopped walking and turned to him. "Oh Gabriel! We have been friends for so many years."

"Friends, yes." There was a sharpness to his tone, which upset her.

"I need your guidance and good thinking." She paused before asking, "As a friend, I welcome your opinion. Should I go?" If she wanted a denial from him, she was disappointed.

"You have little choice if your husband demands it. I shall do my best in your absence to curb any excesses by my brother, in his position as reeve, and I am happy to work closely with Sir Rogier should he wish it."

"I intend to speak with him and I shall tell him to trust your judgement. His heart is at the castle rather than here, but he will understand the need to spend more time around the manor while I am away."

"Very well, my lady. If that is all? I have tasks to fulfil."

"Yes, of course, Gabriel. Thank you. That will be all."

He gave her a formal bow before turning and striding across the grass, his back as straight as a pike staff and full of tension. She watched him go towards the kitchen gardens with a heavy heart. Was he going to see Avice? Possibly. She shouldn't resent that, but she did.

Gariel strode across the grass under the fruit trees. His mind was on what Elizabeth had said. As a 'friend' she asked his advice. He entered the kitchen gardens through the small wicker gate that separated it from the orchard.

"Good day, Master Smith." A female voice floated across the beds of sprouting vegetables and herbs. He looked up and saw Avice smiling at him. "Why so serious?"

"I'm on my way to the barns. It's quicker this way. What are you collecting?" It was a needless question as he could see well what was in her basket.

"I said I would help Cook as she is short-staffed today. Young Mavis has a mild ague. Cook gave her a mix of stale ale, ground nutmeg and mustard seeds. She'll soon be right." Avice laughed. "Anyone would be right soon enough if they had to drink that."

Her voice was high-pitched, not as melodious as Elizabeth's was, but he smiled back at her. "Indeed. I remember having similar as a child."

Avice glanced up at him from under her long dark lashes. He didn't miss the look she flashed at him, or the inference in her voice when she said, "If you were poorly, Master Gabriel, I'd give you something better than that, for sure."

He laughed with her. "Are you finished here? Let me carry that for you."

She handed him the basket and they chattered comfortably enough all the way back to the kitchen door, where he returned her load and bade her good day.

At midday only Elizabeth, Mary and Isabelle sat at the table to eat. Making light conversation, Elizabeth asked Mary, "Is Sir Bartholomew out riding again?"

"Yes, he said he was going to exercise his hawk with that man from Sempringham who is staying as his guest. Another odious creature."

Isabelle said nothing but gave a small nod of agreement before flicking a glance across to the maidservant. Avice stepped forward with the jug ready to pour more wine.

"I believe I shall be accompanying Alaric to London before long," Elizabeth said, searching around for something to say to alleviate the heavy atmosphere.

"No! You cannot!" Mary's voice was loud in the silence of the great hall.

Elizabeth was taken aback by her mother's reaction and Isabelle gasped in surprise.

"You cannot go and leave me here alone," Mary said with quiet urgency.

Elizabeth frowned. "But you are not alone, Mother. You have Sir Bartholomew to protect you and a house full of guards and servants. Isabelle is here, too. Anyway, from whom do you need protection?"

If she thought Mary would accuse her husband, of course, she was wrong.

"I … I… Never mind. I spoke without thought."

"If Sir Alaric asks me to go, and I believe he will, I must accompany him. I am his wife. In truth, it would be exciting to see all of which I have heard so much."

"Yes. A wife must do as her husband commands, I know this," Mary said, before adding in a whisper, "only too well."

Elizabeth glanced at Isabelle, who kept her eyes lowered.

"I intend to speak to Rogier. I am certain that Lady Katherine will understand if he needs to be here in my absence. She may also go to court and thus his presence in Folkingham will be needed less anyway."

At this, Isabelle looked up and smiled. "We shall do very well, Mother, especially if Sir Rogier is here," she said.

There were occasions when Elizabeth and Alaric's ride south had been smooth, as they passed fields, rivers and small villages, but overall the journey had been long and arduous, with the bumping of the carriage on the rutted tracks jarring every bone. The outriders had ensured their safety, for some roads passed through forests where thieves could lie in wait. The inns at which they changed horses and had stayed were generally clean and they had eaten well. Alaric's generous payments ensured as much.

They entered London through the Cripplegate in the north side of the old Roman walls. As the carriage passed through the thick stone walls of the city, everything changed. Houses and shops crowded next to one another and there were people everywhere. Elizabeth hardly knew which way to look first. There was an air of urgency that she had not witnessed before, as people seemed bent on one mission or another. One impatient man pushing a handcart shouted at another for crossing too close in front of him. A woman with several children in tow turned to berate them for dawdling too far behind, her expression reflecting her mood. She saw a dog running with a huge bone in its mouth, though from where he might have stolen it, Elizabeth did not see.

"What is that building?" she asked, pointing at a grand façade. "Surely, it must be a palace."

"That's the Guild Hall," replied Alaric. "It's where our taxes are delivered by the sheriffs who travel all around the country, and then it is counted on an enormous chequered cloth. The squares on the cloth acts as an abacus. The Guild Hall is known as the exchequer these days because of that cloth."

Elizabeth nodded, but her avid gaze had already moved on. On every corner there appeared to be a church or other religious building: St Mary Magdalene, All Hallows, St Thomas of Acon, St Mary's. Then they turned and before long they were following the path of the mighty River Thames towards their destination. They passed Blackfriars where the Dominican monks were housed then, passing over the Fleet River, Elizabeth held a posey of dried herbs to her nose. "Oh, that's noisome."

Alaric nodded. "Yes, it carries much human effluent from houses, and the sewage from the prison. Its waters mix with urine from the tanneries. There is a move to ban such practice from within the city walls as they have done with butchery, which must now be done outside. There are laystalls on the riverbank here, too, where refuse and animal dung are deposited. Five barges located downstream take it away with regularity." He turned to point. "Look, there is Whitefriars."

Elizabeth saw another magnificent building. "It's very large compared to our own Vaudey Abbey."

"The Carmelites had the sympathy of Richard, Duke of Cornwall who was brother to King Henry III. The building was extended vastly more than a hundred years ago and still remains. The church is being rebuilt again now."

"You know so much," commented Elizabeth.

"I have visited before."

They progressed to The Strand, where they passed some very grand houses.

"Our own Lord John is housed only a stone's throw from the Savoy Palace," Alaric said with pride.

"The Savoy? Is that Lord John of Gaunt, Duke of Lancaster's palace?"

Alaric smiled at her naivety. "Yes, my dear."

"I heard he is the richest man in the land," she whispered, although there was no one else to hear her excitement. "Will we see him?"

"I'm sure we shall, but probably only from a distance and yes, he is by far the most wealthy." Alaric lowered his voice. "And he strives to ensure he is the most powerful, too. Both he and another of the king's uncles, Lord Thomas of Woodstock, are determined to rule through the young king, but *do not* speak of this at court. Thereby lies the route to ruin, Elizabeth."

As he went about his business, Gabriel could not help but think about Elizabeth and what she would be doing. He wondered if she would be safe in the city so far away, and so foreign to everything about which she knew.

He had heard that plague erupted regularly in pockets of dense population, and following the Great Mortality there was always the genuine fear it would take hold again. Pickpockets and thieves still practiced. Rumours of intrigue, infighting and instability among the highest ranks were rife and stories spread to even the smallest hamlets via wandering players and travelling salespeople. Gabriel ensured he was well-informed and frequently spoke with the monks at Vaudey Abbey who had the latest information. He sent silent prayers for Elizabeth's safety.

With Elizabeth's marriage, and the business of their departure, the issue of Master Pullen's non-payment of the merchet for his sister had slipped, but Gabriel was keen to pursue the matter. He had managed to persuade Marcus to relinquish the problem to himself, saying it would be one less thing for him to deal with, especially with the busy time ahead. He also suggested that it could be controversial and Marcus must think of his position as reeve, which would be up for discussion prior to renewal at the end of September.

He was pleased when Marcus came to him the next day and said, "Perhaps you might pursue this problem with Master Pullen. I am particularly busy at the moment and need to be on top of all farming-related issues."

"Of course, Brother, leave it with me," Gabriel had said.

Only a few days passed before Sir Rogier spoke to Gabriel. "I have a message back regarding Master Pullen. Indeed, his sister died last winter of a malaise of the chest. He owes nought of the merchet for her. He may be released from house arrest and return to work. Could you deliver the news, Master Smith?"

Now, as he strode along the track towards the village to visit to the sokeman, Gabriel saw Marcus talking with Sir

Bartholomew, who was mounted on a fine steed. Gabriel bowed his head to the master and greeted his brother as he drew level.

"I shall only be gone for a day, so ensure those thistles down in Kerchief Field are dealt with before I return," Sir Bartholomew said.

"Yes, sir. I know of it and instructed a working group yester morn." Marcus turned to Gabriel. "Good day to you, Brother."

Sir Batholomew glanced at Gabriel without formal acknowledgement, then kicked his horse to ride on.

"What did he want?" asked Gabriel when he had gone.

"He's away to see a relative," replied Marcus. "A cousin near his old home who he has heard is nearing death. In fact, this person is also a cousin of his wife, Lady Mary. He needs to ensure the cousin's soul is paid for if they do die, and their property disposed."

"He'll resent paying the tithe. A tenth of his possible inheritance?" The brothers smiled at each other in understanding. "The rector there may take it in seeds or good but perhaps he'll be fortunate and it may be woodland."

"Yes, then it would be nothing owed. A cousin also of Lady Mary's? Must be several times removed."

Gabriel frowned. Something Marcus had said had got him thinking. He would visit Master Pullen to inform him that he was relieved of the accusation against him, and then he would go to the abbey to make further enquiries regarding a particular law. The information he sought would be there, for sure.

As Gabriel went on his way he began to whistle. If he was correct, then he had the answer to a number of problems.

CHAPTER 15

Gabriel skirted King John's Tower, built by Gilbert de Gant more than two hundred years previously, and rounded the wall that housed the men who lived and served there to protect the castle's estates. It was a useful outpost in case of attack along the Great North Road to the west, and the north-south route to Lincoln also ran past its doors. As he descended from the outpost towards the sinuous little valley now called Vaudey, he could see the abbey through the trees. The name had changed over the years as it had grown in size and importance, though Gabriel well understood why it was originally called Vallis Dei. It was indeed God's valley, with its alders and willows and the little river that fed the stew ponds for the fish upon which the monks relied for their diet. Built from the same limestone as the manor and King John's Tower, the abbey was familiar and much loved.

This region was his home and Gabriel had no wish to explore London or across the sea as Sir Alaric, and presumably Sir Rogier, did. If he could not have Elizabeth then this would have to suffice — his homeland. Here he would be content to protect her as much as any knight in battle, and he'd ensure she was safe from any home-grown foe, too. His mission to the abbey might help guarantee her family's happiness and security if what he suspected to be true could be proven. First, however, he must verify the law for himself.

Gabriel entered the abbey church. The incense from the daily services assailed his nostrils. He looked around at the colourfully painted walls full of stories from the Bible. Then his eyes roamed up at the soaring space above him and the great, black oak beams supported by angels trumpeting their silent song. He heard the heavy clang of metal as the door opened, followed by the deep, familiar voice of Father Prior in the cavernous space.

"My son, what brings you here?"

"Father." Gabriel bowed his head, acknowledging the eminence before him. "I hoped you might be free at this hour to give me advice."

"Certainly. Let us walk among the trees where we shall not be overheard. It is peaceful there and you seem troubled."

Gabriel was grateful for the immediacy of his understanding, but he was unsurprised. As they walked beside the stream and heard the burbling of the shallow water over its stones Gabriel took courage from the sound. He had known Father Prior since childhood and had certainty that this man would treat his enquiries with utmost confidence.

Their feet crunched on the dried leaves, and Father Prior waited for Gabriel to speak.

"I am concerned for the Lady Mary, and Elizabeth is worried, too. Excuse me, I mean Lady Elizabeth," he corrected himself with haste.

The elderly monk nodded. "I know how it lies with you, my son. I have seen the way you look at the daughter of the manor. I may not have been fully in the world for many years but I have had the privilege of observing it for all that time."

Gabriel allowed a small smile to twitch his lips.

"But it is advice with regard to Lady Mary you seek?" the monk prompted.

"Yes, that is so." Gabriel hesitated. "Though it is difficult for one in my position to say."

"You think Lady Mary made a poor match when she married Master de Ath?"

Gabriel looked at him in surprise. "It's not for me to judge her decision, but I see she is unhappy and sometimes, well … sometimes she has bruises and the other day she could not move her arm without pain."

Father Prior nodded and paused a moment. "A husband may do as he pleases, but Sir Batholomew has a short temper. More, I do not think he is getting as much as he thought he might from this marriage. I mean in a material sense, of course, and perhaps in other ways, too."

Gabriel said nothing, he had no need. From times past he knew the old man at his side liked to consider little scandals and idle prattle about the people in his care. It was not done with malice but having listened he often had wise words to impart, especially if the situation was more serious, as was this. It seemed he had heard or seen exactly what was happening.

They walked on in silence for several minutes before the venerable man spoke again. "I was surprised they were allowed to marry," he said, with a glance at Gabriel. "Lady Mary herself has been to see me, asking for my counsel."

Gabriel took a sharp intake of breath. "Please don't imagine I wish to interfere, Father. It is only out of concern that I have approached you."

"I'm pleased you have." They stopped walking and the monk put his hand on Gabriel's forearm. "I think Lady Mary may need your help."

"What should I do? As you say, she must submit to the will of her husband. The Church will not allow divorce, unless…"

"Exactly, unless… They are nobility, my son. Well, Lady Mary is."

"And the rules of Pope Urban VI must be observed?" Gabriel bowed his head and made the sign of the cross. "This is what I came to clarify."

"Yes, indeed. More so for the middle ruling classes than for the populace. Or for kings and the exceedingly rich," he added. "Sir Batholomew gained permission for the marriage from those who rule nearer to his own home. These people would only know what he told them."

"Are you talking about consanguinity, Father?"

"I am. Before 1215 marriage between sixth cousins was disallowed. It was considered incestuous."

"But that cannot be the case now, surely? Almost everyone would be disbarred, for with such a law almost everyone would be related too closely."

"When the Fourth Lateran Council clarified the issue they changed the status, too, because, as you say, almost every local inhabitant is related in some way if you go back far enough." He chuckled. "They reduced the prohibited degrees of consanguinity for marriage from seven to four. This meant that a marriage between individuals who shared a common ancestor no more than four generations back was prohibited and required a special dispensation from the Church."

"Sir Bartholomew said he was going to see a cousin today, who is also a cousin of his wife."

The old man nodded.

"When Edward of Woodstock married Joan of Kent, were they not first cousins only once removed?" Gabriel had heard that Edward of Woodstock, father of their present king, had a scandalous marriage but that the Pope allowed it.

"Yes, and they actually married before the permission arrived, but it was never fully accepted by many."

Gabriel shook his head to clear his thoughts. "Are you suggesting that Lady Mary might have married with falseness?"

"She was innocent, I am sure. Her head is sometimes muddled by all with which she cannot manage. This was especially so after her father Sir Ruadhán died."

Gabriel nodded. This clarified what he hoped, but how he would approach it, he knew not. Clearly he must consult Elizabeth.

They turned to retrace their steps. Gabriel spoke first. "Thank you, Father."

"Have a care, my son. You are an asset to the manor and all would suffer should you lose your post as bailiff."

"Yes, Father." Gabriel's heart was heavy. He must slow down and consider with prudence.

As they prepared to say their farewells, Gabriel knelt among the trees. The light stippled the forest floor and the air was sweet with birdsong as he received the blessings that his soul craved. When he stood, he kissed the ring of office and set off with greater serenity but much to consider. He wondered how long Elizabeth would be away. Was she liking her different situation among the richest and most landed in the country? Surely it would not turn her head and alter her priorities.

Elizabeth's gazed around in astonishment at Westminster Palace. The clock tower built by their present king's grandfather, Edward III, stood tall to the north of the Great Hall.

"It's huge," she said, her voice quiet with reverence.

"This palace is the heart of secular and also ceremonial life these days, my dear," Alaric said. It occurred to her he sounded pompous, something she had not noticed previously. Perhaps it was only that he had seen these things before and she had not. Generously, she allowed him his superiority, for in this she could not deny he had the experience.

Elizabeth glanced at him and noted his expression of admiration. "Our own King Richard was accompanied here by his lords and nobles from the Tower before his coronation. He uses this palace above all his others."

While there were innumerable windows denoting many rooms in the building, the Great Hall was even more than she expected. At one end was the dais at which the king would be seated and where his royal table ate their meals. There was a canopy above which melded royal and religious imagery. All others were to be seated on a lower level, as they were for Elizabeth and Alaric's wedding feast at their own manor This was different by its sheer size. It took Elizabeth's breath as she gazed around the walls, and up at the high ceiling.

Alaric leaned in to whisper in her ear. "The first parliament was held here almost a hundred years ago."

"It's enormous. I feel like a tiny mouse in here."

"It's the largest hall in Europe, the walls being over six feet in thickness. King William, of days past, wanted it even larger."

Elizabeth blinked. "And the king is here?" she asked.

"Yes, he is in residence. He was at Sheen Manor briefly, but now he is here."

"Shall we see him?"

"I'm sure we shall be able to watch him at his food. Our own Lord John requested my presence, so I may be even closer at times. After all, the privy council will meet here and Lord John may want me to tend him."

Elizabeth took a breath. She would not gain such an honour, of course, but she would hear all about it.

The noise of so many people speaking at once as they milled about and greeted each other was almost deafening. Clothing was vibrant and jewels sparkled. King Richard himself was a leader of fashion and encouraged bright colours and rich fabrics. Many men wore a cotehardie in silk with pied or diagonal bars of coloured silk. Belts and pouches were emblazoned with squares of precious metals. Some men, and women also, wore a longer houppelande with flowing sleeves richly embroidered or adorned with heraldic symbols and lined with fur. Most of the men wore their hair long, since they were not expected to engage in battle again yet, and flowers made in gold or enamel encircled their heads. Elizabeth wore her best peacock-coloured gown but still felt provincial. Now she was married, her hair was tucked into a gold net caul albeit decorated with some precious stones Alaric had purchased especially for the visit.

She wished Lady Katherine were here to keep her company and show her the way. Fortunately, her awkwardness did not last long, for as they stood behind the benches waiting to be seated for their meal, she had the opportunity to speak with a young lady who was also accompanying her husband to court for the first time. The young woman introduced herself as Alice, Lady Lovering, from Essex. Another, who stood on her other side, leaned across and introduced herself as Lady Jane. This lady was from Kent and having been to court before, she said, Elizabeth judged her to be about ten years older.

A herald announced the arrival of the king and his table. Elizabeth saw a young man of unusual height, though slight in frame. His moustache and beard was hardly visible, being only thirteen years of age, though as he strode into the hall with presence and purpose. Here was a young man, Elizabeth thought, who relished ceremony and the finer things. His clothes were rich in colour and stylish. He had jewels at his neck and on his fingers, and a circlet of gold sat on his fair, wavy-haired head.

He was followed by several older men and there was a stir among the crowd as one in particular readied to take his place as soon as the king was seated.

"That's the Duke of Lancaster, John of Gaunt," Lady Jane whispered close to Elizabeth's ear. Then she added, "He embraces much controversy."

The duke was a man of imposing height and broad shoulders with grizzled hair reflecting his age. He reminded Elizabeth of a great wolf, about which she had heard skulked on the battlefields at the end of the fight, though this man would never skulk for rich pickings. He walked with the arrogance and confidence of the king's uncle who had led the boy thus far and was rich beyond most people's imagination.

"I'm surprised he's here. I heard he was travelling north to the Marches of Scotland." Elizabeth tried to sound more knowledgeable than she was.

"He will leave in the next few days to join his friend, of whom he can be certain of more loyalty than elsewhere," Jane whispered. "Let's hope he has a more dazzling time there than he did in France."

Elizabeth was shocked at this forthright opinion, although of course she knew he'd had little success across the Channel in the last few years.

"What friend?" She glanced around to see if they might have been overheard.

"The Lord of Alnwick recently granted the Earldom of Northumberland. No wonder he's loyal. His son Henry, the one they call 'Hotspur', might be another matter. He's headstrong, though brave in battle, they say."

Elizabeth turned her head to speak to Lady Alice, hoping it would be a less contentious conversation, but her gaze was inexorably drawn back to the lord who gained his name from his birthplace of Ghent. He was an imposing man, ensuring Elizabeth could not rationalise the idea that he was the offspring of a butcher, as rumour had it, rather than the third and oldest surviving son of King Edward III. He was a handsome man. Elizabeth could see, even from this distance, that he held great charm, but also a determination showed in his face as his gaze challenged everyone in the room.

"Is that his wife, the Lady Constance, beside him?" Elizabeth asked her new young friend.

"Oh no!" Jane leaned in and gave a low-throated chuckle. "That, my dear, is Lady Katherine Swynford. He may have come by the vast land of the Duchy of Lancaster from his first wife, Blanche, and now also Lincoln and Leicester upon the death of her sister, but this one has brought him four children, and in quick succession, too. Clearly he still visits Lady Katherine at her house in Lincoln since she was brought to bed for the fourth time by him just last year."

"But I thought he was married to Lady Constance from Castile?"

"That was simply a dynastic arrangement, though he is having trouble wresting her lands from a rival claimant, Henry of Trastámara." She chuckled again. "He's still the richest man in the kingdom and he does hold the dukedom of Aquitaine, as well. No, Lady Katherine is simply governess to his girl children from Blanche. That's what they say, anyway."

Two days later and Elizabeth was beginning to understand the way of life at court. Much time was spent in the ladies' solar and she was expected to make progress with her embroidery. She found the hours tedious and the women tended to talk about others of whom she knew little or nothing. There was also much talk of Lord Gaunt and his domestic arrangement. Presumably, they were safe to do this since Katherine Swynford had returned to her house in Lincoln and the Duke of Lancaster had left for his travels north.

"I believe he loved Lady Blanche with desperation and utter loyalty," one lady said.

Another made the sign of the cross as she spoke. "God bless and keep her soul. Indeed, he must. It will be why he has had that extravagant tomb commissioned in Old St Paul's for them to share after he departs this world."

"This marriage with Lady Constance is completely different from what I saw before," an older lady said. "For twenty years he's had almost an obsession to rule as King of Iberia and he hoped to do that through her and Castile.

"Fornicator and adulterer they call him."

"Hush! Be careful what you say. Anyway, you could not be more wrong. He genuinely loves Lady Swynford. He is loyal and caring. You only have to watch them together."

"No matter what rumours circulate, he is committed to King Richard's success as he was to the king's father, his own brother. He used to follow Prince Edward around like a dog. Even to war," the older lady said.

"There was ten years between them. Hero worship, I suppose."

Elizabeth followed the conversation as it moved around the room, fascinated to learn more of their benefactor, for Lord John and those on her own estate were Lancaster men, through and through. Lord Gaunt's son, Henry, cousin to the king, was born and lived at Bolingbroke Castle close to their own lands in Lincolnshire.

At that moment the voices fell silent as the door opened. Elizabeth could not contain her joy and leapt from her chair as she saw who it was. Lady Katherine Beaumont breezed into the room, a vision in swirling red, gold and green as a reference to the coronation colours of the young King Richard. She brought with her a breath of freshness and vitality.

Holding out both hands to the newcomer Elizabeth said, "I'm so incredibly pleased to see you. A loyal friend and familiar face at last."

"And I, you. I'm pleased to be here. I love the country but I miss all this." She swept her arms out to encompass the whole room. "Good day, ladies, I am newly come from Lincolnshire and pleased to re-acquaint with you all." Then she took Elizabeth's hand and pulled her towards the door. "Come to my private rooms. I want to hear all the latest news and also how you are enjoying it here at court."

Lady Katherine's rooms were comfortable and not unlike those allotted to Elizabeth and Alaric in style. The main difference was she had her own suite as wife of a Privy Councillor and an important man in the king's retinue. It transpired during the conversation that while her husband had a room for when he was working late in the government chamber, he also had his own luxurious dwelling in London not far from Westminster, though nothing like the grandeur and size of the Duke of Lancaster's Savoy Palace.

"This is all so impressive," Elizabeth said.

"You should see the Painted Chamber where the business of government is discussed," Katherine said. "It was originally the King's Chamber with a great canopied bed but now it's used for parliamentary discussions."

"Why is it called the Painted Chamber?" Elizabeth asked.

"It takes its name from a series of large paintings which decorate the walls; the profusion of colours is quite remarkable." She lowered her voice, "I hear the young King Richard loves to see himself enthroned with his lords around him. It's almost sacrilegious. Some day he will either be a magnificent ruler in his own right, away from his uncles, or he will overstep things and fall from a great height. Do not repeat what I say, Elizabeth. I never voice such thoughts in public." She laughed and the mood lightened.

At this point Elizabeth asked to know what was happening at home. She suddenly longed to be there, in the fields, or under the trees, away from all this intrigue and gossip. An image of Gabriel with his dark hair and azure eyes inveigled itself. She ached for the comfort of a conversation with him, for a shared joke, for the easy teasing that had developed between them, before her marriage.

CHAPTER 16

Gabriel missed Elizabeth. He lay awake at night and found it hard to concentrate during the day. His temper was short for he missed her presence around the manor. He was so used to seeing her lithe figure striding along footpaths, bending to speak with a child of one of the cottars, issuing orders and discussing the season's work with him.

Frequently, he saw Avice around the manor and each time he contemplated a future with her as his wife. Though she was pretty and his if he wished, he couldn't quite bring himself to make that step. Yet Elizabeth could never be his.

The meetings with Rogier, now that he was home, were satisfactory, and while the young man understood most of the routines, he lacked any depth of interest. Frequently, it was Gabriel who sensitively guided the conversation about what needed to be done and then he would issue the orders or speak to his brother, the reeve. Sometimes when he sought out the young sir, he was nowhere to be found until it transpired he had gone to the lists to practice his skills there.

Gabriel ensured he always appeared subservient to Master Bartholomew, but quietly went about his work while watching what that man was up to. He did not trust him. When he had a free day, he determined to travel to the village of the cousin's dwelling and ask around about other members of the family. If he could prove a closer relation to Lady Mary than was proper it would give Elizabeth power to act, should it become necessary. The last time he had seen Lady Mary she had averted her face with speed, but not before Gabriel had seen a livid bruise under one eye. Gabriel made the connection to a conversation he had overheard the previous day.

"You will not," Sir Bartholomew had said in a tone that brooked no argument.

The man had not taken notice of Gabriel as he passed through the hall. Gabriel was on his way to see the pantler but lingered in the shadows where the screen separated the hall from the corridor to the kitchens and the pantry.

"But I only wanted to go and see..." Mary's voice was timorous.

"You heard me, Wife. You will not!"

"Very well, sir. May I go to my solar now?"

"Yes. Leave me. Take your whining tone and your pasty face away."

Gabriel saw Mary curtsey before she scuttled away across the rushes. He turned in the shadows and continued on his own mission.

Once or twice, Gabriel saw Isabelle, either at table or walking in the gardens. She never maintained conversation with her father for long. On one occasion he saw them together in the courtyard. "I'm going riding," Bartholomew said. "Why not accompany me? I bought you that little horse. It cost me eighty shillings. That, my girl, is nearly half a year's wages for one of the men in the village."

"I have things to do, Father. I did not ask for such a mount. I do not enjoy riding out."

"It's a palfrey, for the dear Lord's sake, not even an ordinary rouncey. You could show some gratitude, Daughter."

"Of course you are generous, sir, with the money of others." Isabelle showed some surprising spirit, Gabriel noted.

Bartholomew raised his hand and she stepped back in haste, nearly tripping on a cobblestone. Gabriel watched as

Bartholomew glanced around, realising he was in the public view. Where he might not be bothered in the house, here there were more people about and several of them could tell Sir Rogier, who might take a tale to Lord John when he returned.

Later that day Gabriel was searching out Sir Rogier when he saw him returning from the direction of King John's Tower. The young squire wore mail over his leather jerkin and his breeches were stained with sweat and oil from the saddle. Below the rim of his small, felted hat, his chestnut hair, so like the colour of Elizabeth's, stuck to his neck. He walked his horse on a leading rein, and beside him walked Lady Isabelle. She looked up at him and laughed at something he said, leaving Gabriel in no doubt where her affections lay. He only hoped she was not doomed for disappointment, for he was certain Sir Bartholomew would not be happy. He would be looking for a greater match for his daughter than the part owner of a manor house, even if he was destined to become a knight before too long.

The image of Elizabeth's hair, remembered from his youth and since, before she married, as he saw her brother now, shot through Gabriel's mind and set his heart pounding.

No wonder the church decrees women should keep it covered. His guilty thoughts did nothing for his comfort or his temper. He wondered for the one thousandth time what she was doing and whether she was safe at the court of King Richard.

In their shared sitting chamber, Alaric spoke to Elizabeth. He welcomed her thoughts and appreciated her sharp mind. She frequently held opinions on matters of state as well as more parochial ideas about running the manor.

"I heard talk another poll tax has been implemented," he said.

"I heard a rumour but I know not from whom." Elizabeth was learning to be circumspect in these opulent surroundings where everyone had an opinion and she was uncertain who reported to whom and about what.

"Before he left for the Marches of Scotland, Lord Gaunt had talks with King Richard. There is little money in the coffers for this dragging war with France."

"The last poll tax was very unpopular and not all paid their dues," said Elizabeth.

"It has been twelve pence per head as an average, but graduated so that the poor paid no more than four pence each."

"For the common people even that amount is difficult to find."

"Even more for us, my dear," said Alaric. "We are subsiding the less wealthy with what we pay. That hardly seems fair."

"Yes, but we pay that without starving ourselves. And why another poll tax? Is there truly talk of increasing it? The Duke, Lord Gaunt, is already facing unpopularity over his support of that religious reformer, John Wycliffe, because he thinks the Church's secular power is too great. Lady Katherine was saying as much just yesterday. This preacher says that all are equal in the eyes of God and that the nobility are not more important than the villeins and serfs. If the Duke of Lancaster is linked to another poll tax this will not go well for him, I fear. Mind you, husband, while the preacher's views risk undoing hundreds of years of social structure, it seems to me he has a point."

"You ladies talk of such matters?" There was surprise in Alaric's tone. "Well, John Wycliffe may be a Catholic priest and seminary professor at Oxford University, but I'm not so sure his radicalism is helping, and for Lord Gaunt to put him above others is reckless. I hope you agree with me, for aught else is insurrection."

Elizabeth decided it was best to change the course of the conversation. "So this other poll tax, what might it be, do you suppose?"

"There is talk of one payment for almost all classes."

"A flat rate? How much, do you think? Have you heard?"

"There is talk of twelve pence for each and all. It will be less complicated and easier to collect."

"Twelve pence? That's outrageous!"

"Hush! Keep your voice down," Alaric said with haste, sounding cross in his sudden fear.

"For people who cannot pay what is levied currently, this will be impossible."

"It's only for those over the age of fifteen."

Elizabeth was exasperated at the foolhardiness of the idea but said no more on it. Instead, her head was full of worry and after several minutes of silence, she ventured in a small voice, "I should like to go home soon."

The next day there was further discussion among the ladies. The subject was rife among everyone, it seemed.

Lady Alice was particularly vocal. "I can tell you this, there are those in my home area who will not stand for it. They are already muttering and grumbling."

"We have that, too," Elizabeth said. "Burgh St Peter is a sizeable town, maybe thirteen hundred people, and has become a place for some to gather, especially since they say the abbey there is too rich with lands around as well as in Lincolnshire and elsewhere."

"I do believe the people of whom I speak, in Essex, may well take it further. There is a man name Jack Rackstraw, or

Rakestraw, he seems to have several names. It's confusing. Sometimes he's referred to as John Wrawe..."

"Never mind that, tell us the story," the older lady interrupted.

Alice blushed. "He preaches in churchyards after the priest has gone. The people are beginning to listen to his wild speeches. He follows the teaching of John Wycliffe and..."

At that moment Lady Jane rushed in. "You'll never guess what I have heard."

All turned to look at the newcomer and hear the latest news.

Lady Jane was unusually flustered. "I must take refreshment. I'm so bothered. One moment, and I shall divulge all."

Ladies stood to bring her a glass of ale, a sweet biscuit, and indicated a seat.

"Tell us, do."

"What is amiss?"

"Is it something to fear?"

The chatter subsided as Lady Jane took a drink and a deep breath, before saying, "A tax collector has been bludgeoned to death."

There were gasps and one lady clutched her chest before sinking down onto a cushion.

"It was so close to my home. I must return as soon as possible, but I fear to travel on the roads without proper guards."

"Tell us what happened," ordered the older lady.

"It's quite shocking. You know this new tax is to be collected from everyone, man or mistress, if they be over fifteen years of age?" said Lady Jane.

"Yes, yes."

"Well, would you believe it. The tax collector only lifted the daughter's skirt to see if she was of an age or not."

A ripple of shock undulated around the room.

"So, the father took the hammer which he was using for his work — he was in the business of placing tiles — and he hit the collector around the head. A mob is gathering and threatening to march on London."

A collective gasp arose.

"There are women among them, too. Feeling is running even higher than it has of late."

At that point several of the women left to find their husbands, including Elizabeth.

Both Elizabeth and Alaric were ready to go home. All their things were placed in trunks, and Elizabeth had pressed some flowers from the gardens as a reminder of her first time at the court of King Richard II. She would place them in her copper treasure box when she returned. They were both relieved that Sir John allowed them to leave.

"I shall miss you," Lady Katherine said to Elizabeth.

"And I you. When you return, we shall have a feast in your honour."

Neither woman knew that they would meet again sooner than expected.

CHAPTER 17

As they rounded the bend in the track and Elizabeth saw the manor for the first time in what seemed an age, her shoulders relaxed. She was home. The grey stones exuded safety and the comfort of familiarity. The clamour and flamboyance of the court in Westminster had been an experience, and she was happy to have had the opportunity to go, but as they neared the bridge over the moat she leaned forward in anticipation.

Alaric sat opposite and she saw his indulgent smile. "I see you are pleased to be home." He sighed. "I fear you did not enjoy your time at court as much as I."

Elizabeth looked at him with a guilty expression. "It was so different, and I'm glad to have seen it all. It's just…"

He laughed. "I understand, Wife."

A messenger had been despatched so all should be ready for their arrival. Where was Gabriel? How was her mother? Had Sir Bartholomew behaved himself? Had the workers undertaken their tasks without grumbling too much? How *was* Gabriel? Unbidden his name returned again and with it an image in her mind of his face, so familiar and much … yes that was the word — loved. Elizabeth peered again from the tiny window cut in the waxed fabric of the covering of the carriage.

At last they rumbled over the bridge and she heard the driver shout "Woah!" as he reined in the horses. Alaric jumped down, followed by Elizabeth, who clambered down from the transport as tidily as she could. That was not done with ease since the chains, aiding a softer ride, ensured the body of the carriage bounced about and it was a deep step down. Alaric offered Elizabeth his hand as chivalry demanded. She looked around. Some of the household were there to welcome them, but not Gabriel. A brief moment of disappointment flitted through her chest like a moth. However, the steward and housekeeper greeted them while others began to empty their baggage cart. As Elizabeth entered the manor, she took a deep breath and revelled in the familiar scents and sights. Lavender and thyme greeted her from among the fresh rushes on the floor. There were new candles in the sconces and a fire crackled in the wide hearth. She stood for a quiet moment, revelling in all she saw.

"Is my brother here?" Elizabeth asked, noting his absence.

"Sir Rogier is at King John's Tower, my lady," the steward answered. "Perhaps he thought you might arrive later. He was eager to practice his horse work. He has news for you, my lady. Grand news."

Alaric jumped into the conversation. "Perhaps I shall ride straight away to greet him, before I change from these travel-soiled clothes." He turned to Elizabeth. "I shall find out what is happening and tell you as soon as I return."

Elizabeth smiled at him, fully understanding the need for her husband to be about knightly enthusiasms. "I shall go to my solar to wash." She turned to the steward. "Is there water waiting?"

"Yes, my lady." It was Avice who stepped forward and prepared to accompany Elizabeth, about which she was happy, for she could ask what had been happening during her absence without fear of favour over truth.

"I have missed my place here among you all," Elizabeth said when she was alone with Avice.

"We are all pleased to have you home, my lady. Especially Master Gabriel."

Elizabeth turned away to remove her wimple, avoiding Avice's look in case she saw the yearning in her eyes, or the blush that she was certain had crept up her cheeks. "Oh?"

"Master Marcus has…" She trailed off.

Elizabeth turned at the uncertainty in Avice's voice. "Master Marcus has what?"

"Gabriel told me he has upset several of the working men with the tasks he has insisted upon. They say it's too much. Gabriel said he would speak to Master Marcus, but that's difficult when Sir Bartholomew has agreed it."

Elizabeth noticed the familiarity with which Avice spoke of Gabriel, but focussed on the news that Sir Batholomew was stirring trouble yet again. She wondered angrily why Rogier was not more involved and concluded that he must have been spending too much time doing what he enjoyed most. It only took a few moments for her to realise she was expecting much from him and the manor had never been his main interest. He made no secret of it. "Do you know any details of the work involved?" she asked.

"No, my lady. Sir Bartholmew discussed matters with Master Marcus while Sir Rogier was away from the manor. It was settled thus, apparently."

Elizabeth stepped over to the wash bowl and changed the subject. "How is my lady mother? I did not see her when we arrived."

"I believe she is well, my lady. I don't see her very often. She spends many hours alone in her rooms. May I speak openly, my lady?"

"I would hope you'd always do that, Avice. You've been here long enough now to know I would always try to be even-handed and I cannot do that with only half of the information."

"Yes, indeed, forgive me. It's simply … well … I see such a sad face on your lady mother. Gabriel confided, in absolute secrecy, my lady, that he believes she is not happy with Sir Bartholomew. He wishes to speak with you about something concerning that."

She would say no more. Elizabeth thanked Avice and she was dismissed. There was much to consider here.

Only a few weeks away from home and several problems had arisen, but the questions that eclipsed all others was why did Gabriel speak in confidence with Avice, and why was she familiar enough to call him by his name without any title?

They must have become close in the weeks she was absent. She could not blame him. Avice was attractive and Gabriel was alone. He was past the age for marrying and he had enough money to sustain a wife and family. Is this why he had been remote with her lately? His attachments were forming with the maidservant? The easy camaraderie between herself and Gabriel had certainly disappeared. She could only suppose because she was married, albeit not a state of her choosing, he had decided to keep his distance, but she mourned the passing of the closeness of their friendship.

With Rogier still not returned from King John's Tower, and Alaric gone to see him, Elizabeth tried to place things in order. She must see Mary first, but did not want to bump into Sir Bartholomew. He was out hunting when she arrived home. She must hope that was still the case. Then she would seek out Gabriel. She must bear being around him even if he was not for her.

The workday dress that Elizabeth had put on over a clean shift was comfortable and she moved with greater ease than in the attire she had worn at court. She went to her mother's solar and knocked. Hearing no response, she called softly, "Mother, 'tis I, Elizabeth, returned and come to see how you are."

She heard a soft, croaky response. "Come in, Daughter, and welcome."

Try as she might, Elizabeth doubted she hid the shock in her expression. A small, huddled figure sat in a chair by the fire. This was some old woman. Not her mother, surely. She was shrouded in clothing that was too large for the emaciated frame and the face that looked up at her was lined with sadness and more. She looked in pain.

Elizabeth knelt by Mary's side and gently took the bony fingers in her own, raising them and placing a kiss there, for she saw how lost this woman had become.

"I have been foolish, my child. I know this now."

"Oh, Mother." Elizabeth's eyes welled up and a lump formed in her throat.

"My head was turned by empty flattery and I acted without thought." Mary bowed her head. "Now I must live with the regret. It is my punishment and must be borne with patience and bravery."

As tears rolled down her cheeks, Elizabeth folded the thin shoulders in her own firm arms and held Mary close.

"We will sort this out, Mother. We will. Rogier and I, together. Ruadhán bade us look after you and we have failed. We will make this right for you."

"I am his wife, child. I must do his bidding and if his … his preferences are not what I expected, I must comply."

"No husband, if he has a jot of chivalry, would ask … things of you, Mother." Elizabeth had no understanding of what her mother spoke, but she could see things were not right with her.

At that moment she heard a commotion downstairs in the hall and guessed her brother had returned. "I shall speak to

Rogier this night and we will amend this situation immediately."

As she reached the bottom of the stairs, Elizabeth commanded Avice to ensure Mary had a warm wine posset. "The cream will benefit her body and the wine her soul. Do not spare the honey, either. The sweetness may help revive her." Then she went to greet Rogier, determined to seek time with him alone to discuss what she had discovered.

Rogier smelled of horses and hard work at the lists. It was not unpleasant, but Alaric excused himself to rinse at the pump and change his clothing. "Tell your sister your news," he said to Rogier upon parting.

Elizabeth seized her chance before it was lost in whatever Rogier had to tell her. "Rogier, I would speak with you about our mother. Our grandfather asked us to care for her and we are failing. I have spoken with her and…"

"And so have I, Sister. I am mindful that things are poor with Master Bartholomew. But what's to do? She married him in haste, without telling us."

"She's becoming ill, Rogier. I'll think about what to do and we'll talk about it further." She took a deep breath. "Now, let me hear your news."

"I am to become knighted!" His voice was loud in his excitement. "Lord John has sent word he is returning, albeit briefly, and my dubbing is to be in the next few days. I am young, he acknowledges, but says I have worked harder than most and am therefore deserving."

Elizabeth clasped his hands together. "Oh Rogier! That is good news indeed. I'm so proud of what you have achieved. It's all through your own determination without father or grandfather to encourage." She meant every word.

At that point Sir Bartholomew returned with his friend, Sir Francis, ordering drink to be sent for. Nodding at Rogier, he greeted Elizabeth. "Lady," he said. "I see you are returned. Has your husband returned also?"

"He has, sir. He will see you when we are at table, later."

With that, the two older men went to sit by the fire.

After giving Rogier a fond embrace, Elizabeth decided to return to her solar. She did not want to share any time with her stepfather and his toady friend.

The following day, Alaric left just after daybreak for the castle at Folkingham to resume his duties there. Rogier had returned to King John's Tower to speak to the master-at-arms and supervise some work. Elizabeth saw Gabriel as she headed for the stables, and he informed her of the news regarding Master Pullen's clearance from charges of non-payment and his subsequent freedom.

"I'm so pleased. He's a good worker and I could not believe he would be such a seditionist, even though he can be outspoken."

She took a pony and rode to the village. It was important to her to check on the welfare of the villagers. The day was fair but a chill wind ensured she had her wool cloak around her shoulders. She nevertheless gloried in the familiarity of the field strips where she saw only a few men at work, which puzzled her. The corn was growing vigorously at this time of year and beginning to outcompete the weeds, but workers were still required to use hoes to ensure the best yield of valuable grain.

Where the longer reeds grew for thatching in the wetter areas, and where drainage ditches needed to be cleared regularly, usually in early spring or in the winter months, there were several groups of three men working. Each had either a badging hook to cut the weeds, a mucking-out fork to throw them up onto the bank, or a spade to dig out the silt. This was the work that was leading to contention with the village men who wanted to work on the production of crops on their own strips of farmland. They didn't need to be there at this time of the year, while the strips of barley, wheat and rye were being neglected. Marcus understood this, so why were they doing it? She thought she recognised the reeve watching them work. She wondered if Gabriel knew of this. She would enquire who had sanctioned such work at this time of year. Perhaps Rogier had agreed it, but it didn't seem right to her.

The first cott she came upon was one of the poorest. The wife was at the door spinning, two young children at her feet. As Elizabeth approached, the woman leapt to her feet and dropped a curtsey. "Good day, my lady," she said.

Elizabeth peeped through the door of the small abode into the gloom. Inside was a single room with a large bed which she knew the whole family would share. The fire was meagre and from the iron tripod hung a pot, but there was no smell of cooking within. The rough-hewn table held a jug and a mortar with its pestle. Two benches sat either side. Some baskets hung from a ceiling beam. There was little else and the floor was hard earth with no comfort of a rug for warmth.

"Good day, Maude," said Elizabeth. "How goes it with you and Gerold?"

"Oh ma'am, things are difficult. Gerold is away ditching today and I should be in the field but had to stay here with the little 'uns. I was badly in the night. It's my stomach. Mayhap somethin' I ate. I told 'im I thought the gruel was off. It was from a few days before, you see. He had none of it so he was all right, but there weren't enough of the bean paste for us all."

"Oh Maude, I'll ensure something is sent over to you as soon as I return to the manor. Why was there not enough bean paste for you as well?"

"Gerold was away ditchin' all week and young Petey was with him, so we hadn't picked enough you see, and the birds had some 'cos Petey wasn't there to scare 'em away."

After her farewells and reiterating she would send some food, Elizabeth visited others. It was a similar story elsewhere, although some houses were empty. Presumably the women were out in the fields with the men.

As Elizabeth returned to the manor house, Marcus crossed her path. He had a working party in tow and they stopped as she approached them, each greeting her politely and bowing their heads.

"Are you going to the fields now?" she asked.

"Not today, my lady," replied Marcus. "There are ditches on the other side still to do."

"What of the weeding of Long Field and Home Field? Has that been done this month?"

Marcus looked shifty and began moving the gravel with the toe of his boot, looking down at his feet as he did so.

"We need to do those, my lady," Master Pullen said. "They didn't get fully done last month either, what with these extra tasks." He shot a dark look at the reeve and Elizabeth understood his meaning.

"You'll have my tongue and more later!" Marcus barked at him. "You will not speak to her ladyship thus. You may have escaped justice this time but be careful!"

Elizabeth was shocked at his tone but she wasn't about to remonstrate with the reeve in front of the men, being well aware that he did not like taking his instructions from her. First, she would consult Rogier and see whose orders these were. "I'm pleased you were found not guilty of the accusations against you, Master Pullen. I heard this morning." She smiled broadly at him but earned a frown from Marcus.

As Elizabeth was returning to the manor, she thought long on her relationship with Gabriel's older brother. He was resentful and did not show her the respect he would have given Rogier. She must search for something and be sure to praise his work soon.

A visitor was leaving as Elizabeth arrived home. He passed her with a cursory nod and sped his horse to a trot, so they did not speak. *He does not realise the position I hold here*, she thought with a degree of resentment. The man rode a fine mount and his clothing looked of superior quality. Who was he?

When she entered the manor house, Bartholomew was leaving the parlour, away from prying ears in the hall. He turned from her as she crossed the rushes and would have avoided her if he could, but her words arrested him.

"Who was that leaving as I arrived? He looked like a gentleman but I wasn't expecting anyone."

"Only some unfinished matter from while you were absent at court. I'm surprised your brother has not told you." He sounded petulant.

"He is busy with Lord John's business since our overlord is due back at Folkingham Castle any day now." She should not have the need to justify their movements. Elizabeth took a deep breath. "Right now, I'm asking you."

Bartholomew held her gaze. "He is a commissioner from the justice court in London. It was a matter of raising the poll taxes and other monies from this demesne. Not all has been paid, it seems. Apparently our own records name the man. It will not surprise you to hear that it is Master Pullen."

"And where is this commissioner going now?"

"To the ditches at the east end of the manor house. No doubt to arrest the offender, and rightly so."

"But surely you told him that Goodwife Pullen is no longer on this earth and he does not owe money for her. The matter has been investigated fully and satisfactorily. I was told this upon my return."

"I did no such thing. I have not been informed. It seems that management is not as good as it should be. Anyway, I will not be party to abusing the laws of the land."

Elizabeth realised she must have a word with the seneschal to ensure their accounts were up to date. Clearly Rogier had omitted to do that.

"I agree, it is not *your* business to know and, as such, you should have given him refreshment and bade him wait for me or Sir Rogier. How dare you interfere and give information that is not correct."

Elizabeth turned angrily and stepped out to find the commissioner and put him right. Then she turned back as a thought struck her. "How do you know they are doing the ditches at the east side of the house? That was no order from me and I doubt very much if it came from Sir Rogier. He knows full well that the crops are of critical importance at this time of year."

"The reeve asked my opinion," Bartholomew blustered, before adding, "in your absence and Sir Rogier's distractions with his work at King John's Tower."

It was quicker for Elizabeth to walk than to wait for a pony to be saddled. She was familiar with the quickest route to the ditches at the east end and grateful that she had chosen to wear her stout boots and workaday dress for visiting the villagers. She increased her speed. All winter and spring, unrest had bubbled. This could be the final straw for discontent among the workers if Master Pullen was wrongly taken.

As she neared the ditches, she saw three men instead of the four she was hoping. Marcus stood with hands on hips, gesticulating every so often.

"Where is Master Pullen?" she demanded of Marcus.

"He has been taken to the prison cell in Burgh St Peter. I imagine he'll be there until the justice of the peace arrives for the next quarter sessions."

CHAPTER 18

Before Elizabeth spoke again with Marcus, Gabriel came to the door and sent a message asking for some of her time.

She bid the maidservant bring him to the parlour. She had ordered a fire lit and the logs crackled with flames, sending warmth through her weary bones. As she sat in a chair to one side, in the quiet privacy of the cosy room, she contemplated her relationship with this man she had known since childhood.

Despite the differences in station, she considered him a friend, a good friend. She was able to talk to him about anything and he would offer sensible advice while respecting her opinion should it differ. When she considered her husband, this was not the case. Alaric's perspectives were that of a knight comparatively newly come to the area and he saw things from a noble's perspective. She wasn't even certain he respected her opinion as he would that of another man. She chastised herself for comparing the two men. Her loyalty should be with Alaric, yet when she saw Gabriel her blood quickened in her veins.

There was a knock on the door and Gabriel stood there. His head was uncovered and his dark hair gleamed in the firelight, his eyes reflecting the dancing flames as he smiled at her. Elizabeth's heart thumped at the sight of him. She cleared her throat and rose from her chair, indicating the one opposite without words, trying to gain some composure.

He bowed and she caught a gentle waft of his masculine scent. It was earthy and honest but there was also a hint of lemons and lavender.

"Shall I call for refreshment?" she asked.

"No, my lady — Elizabeth," he corrected himself, remembering her previous admonishment for using her title. "There are several matters I would discuss with you but I know you are busy so perhaps I might speak."

Gabriel heard his own voice as it became husky. "I... We've missed you, while you were at the king's court." How he longed to take her hand to tell her how much he had missed her. He had missed the sound of her voice, and the sight of her swaying hips as she strolled beneath the trees in the orchard. He had imagined her reaching up and taking the twigs between her slender fingers to smell the blossom. He had missed her melodious tones as she greeted people on her way to the stables. He physically ached when he thought of the privileges her husband enjoyed, and he could not. He considered Avice. She was comely and he was certain she liked him. Since Elizabeth was out of his reach, perhaps he should ask permission to marry the maid.

"What did you wish to see me about, for there are things I would ask of you while we are here together?"

Here together, he thought. *And yet not together, not at all.*

Gabriel dragged his thoughts back to the moment. "May I speak openly about your stepfather?" he said.

"I entreat you to do so. Master Bartholomew has been causing Rogier and I much trouble and I am despairing."

"What has he done now?" he leaned forwards in his chair.

She told him briefly of the recent arrest of Master Pullen and how she was certain it was Sir Bartholomew's meddling that had caused it.

"But I found out the truth of the accusations. The sister has indeed passed away and Master Pullen owes nothing."

"Sir Bartholomew claimed he had not been told, so when the commissioner arrived he was unable to say it. I'm not sure I believe him, but it may be so. Marcus would have known, however, and chose not to speak out. He has his own grievances with Master Pullen — and me." She shrugged and he saw a half smile, as if this was the least of her concerns.

"I did tell Marcus, after I had informed Sir Rogier. I didn't think it necessary to tell Sir Bartholomew as well, believing it was not his responsibility. I'm so sorry if I have been remiss and caused you a further problem."

"No, no." She waved aside his concern. "Maybe Rogier decided it was none of our stepfather's business since that man has no responsibility for this manor and its people. But tell me, what of your news?"

"I have made some enquiries both at the abbey and towards Sempringham, where Sir Bartholomew originates. It came to me that he said he was visiting a cousin who is also a cousin of Lady Mary."

"A cousin to both?"

Gabriel nodded. "I see you are ahead of me."

"I know naught of such a relationship, but should it be the case then how can they be married in law? If Sir Bartholomew knew this he should have declared as much."

"In fact, he should not have asked Lady Mary to wed in the first place. It's one thing for kings and noblemen, but not for regular folk, even landed gentry."

"Is this grounds for an annulment?" Elizabeth leaned forwards in her chair. "Rogier and I know he is cruel, yet she says she must obey her husband. She looks ill these days and has withdrawn from all life at the manor. I am worried for her; she is vulnerable and not strong."

"Perhaps it's something to discuss with her. You might ask her if she wishes to stay in this relationship if it does not comply with the law. I understand she has spoken with Father Prior of her unhappiness."

"I didn't know that." Elizabeth was silent for a moment, contemplating all he had said. "I shall speak with my brother and then with Lady Mary. I cannot thank you enough for this information, Gabriel."

"If Sir Bartholomew set out to deceive and did not declare this relationship, then..." He shrugged. "I suppose he came from far enough away for it to remain thus."

A log slipped, sending sparks flying up the chimney. It brought them back to the moment.

"Perhaps back to this other matter — Master Pullen's arrest?" Elizabeth said.

"I fear this could cause serious unrest. I heard news yesterday of a major riot not so far from here, at a place called Fobbing in the county of Essex. Apparently, a royal commissioner came enquiring about non-payment of the poll tax."

Elizabeth frowned. "The same as with Master Pullen."

"Yes, although this one's methods were brutal. One Thomas Baker has led a group of men who put him to rout."

"Who? The royal commissioner?"

"Indeed."

"That is a major offence and very dangerous."

"Baker is a man of some intelligence with property of six acres or more, not a landless vagrant who has acted without consideration. He has become a leader of men who are discontented with the way the poll tax is demanded equally from all, whether they are landed or poor. They are also noisy about the Statute of Labourers setting the maximum wage, even when there is a shortage of labour and poaching of men from one estate to another. The poor are staying poor. Elizabeth, this is serious. I know you supplement the peasants' food and do what extra you can, but the law is a foolish mule."

"I would welcome your advice about the return of Master Pullen. They are departed already for Burgh St Peter and that's a day's ride, at least."

"Yes, it's too late now. Perhaps I might have letters to take and I could go tomorrow to gain his release, if that would sit well with you?"

"That would be a great relief." Elizabeth paused before continuing. "Perhaps I should speak with my brother first, and you go the day after. All should be well until then, don't you think?"

"Yes, I'm sure. It will be another few weeks before the next quarter sessions and a decision made, and while we don't want Master Pullen to suffer longer than necessary, if a missive had your Sir Rogier's signature, as well as your own, it would carry full weight."

Elizabeth could not deny that her signature alone, that of a woman, would not be as strong.

"Perhaps I may take my leave," said Gabriel, standing. "I wish to find my brother. Marcus owes me an explanation for why he was not more explicit with the truth."

"I imagine he was taking his lead from Sir Bartholomew. You have my most sincere thanks, Gabriel." She reached out to touch his arm but he saw her hesitation before her hand withdrew.

"It is my pleasure," he replied formally.

It was a busy time for Rogier so when Elizabeth asked to speak with him on urgent business he was impatient.

"Sister, I have to prepare for my dubbing. You know this. Surely it can wait a day or two."

"It cannot. I understand this is indeed a momentous time, but the shadows are still long and the morn is yet young. Please? It's important and might affect our mother deeply." She took a pace towards the house, hoping he would follow her across the courtyard and into the hall.

Rogier carefully placed the equipment he was carrying on the stone mounting block, before calling to a lad to watch his things. They were valuable and he had spent many hours cleaning and preparing all. "And don't let any horse spin mud from its hooves nearby." He leaned close to the young serf and added, "If all is well when I return, I'll give you a groat."

As soon as they were out of earshot, Elizabeth spoke. "I have learned from Gabriel about the close family relationship Sir Bartholomew has with our lady mother, even before he took her for his wife." She explained what she had been told about the cousins and reiterated the law, as it stood. "Gabriel verified the fact and spoke with Father Prior at the monastery."

"Why did he not come to me first?"

"He knows how busy you are," Elizabeth said with tact, "and he wished to verify the facts. But the point is that Bartholomew de Ath deceived us *and* the priest who married them. This is most definitely grounds for an annulment. But first we must speak with Mother."

"Yes, we must do that." Rogier paused in thought. "She may not wish him gone, of course."

"No, she may not, but he is cruel to her and she is no longer sprightly and mirthful."

"You are right, Sister. I cannot remember the last time I saw her smile, never mind laugh."

"When will you be free to speak with her?"

"Me?"

"Both of us together, Rogier. This is not something I should do alone."

"No, of course. You're right."

"I think it should be as soon as possible. This afternoon? Bartholomew will be out riding. It's his habit, especially since his friend, Sir Francis, is here."

"Very well, I shall return by the bells of sext for our midday meal and then stay for an interview with our mother. You must ensure she is alone and in her solar."

"I shall."

"Now, before I leave for King John's Tower, perhaps I might have a word with Gabriel. Where might he be?"

"He awaits a word also. This is the other matter of import. You know Gabriel verified that Master Pullen owed no tax for his sister who is deceased? Well, he has since been taken into custody and it's not right. It seems that Marcus saw fit to say nothing when the king's commissioner came to either reclaim the money or take the culprit. My view is he was obeying orders given by our stepfather. I have prepared letters for Gabriel to take to Burgh St Peter."

Rogier made to rise up in anger from the wooden settle upon which they sat.

"Hold, Brother." Elizabeth placed her hand on his arm. "If Bartholomew must leave then that situation should set itself aright. In the meantime, let us go to the parlour and perhaps you might read the missive I have prepared, and sign it to secure the release of Master Pullen."

Together they stood and made their way across the hall to the parlour. Rogier took the letter Elizabeth had scribed in her own hand.

Later, after they had eaten, the conversation with Mary was delicate and interlaced with tears. "He said it was perfectly lawful and told me of the king's father, Edward, who married his first cousin."

"Yes, but they had a special dispensation from Pope Urban. It is unlikely that Sir Bartholomew would have received such a valued thing, even if he had asked, which I am certain he did not, considering the haste in which he churched you." Elizabeth sat at Mary's side, holding her hand.

Rogier was blunt. "Mother, the man is a charlatan who thought he could marry you and achieve greater status by ruling these manor lands."

There was a loud sob. "I couldn't manage on my own after your father died and left us. Then, when I was without a parent, too, well…"

"We understand, Mother," soothed Elizabeth. "But now we see you careworn and unhappy. You have hinted that Sir Bartholomew mistreats you."

Mary shot a look at Elizabeth before dabbing her face with her sleeve. "He is my husband; I must obey him."

Rogier took a deep breath. "If he took your hand when there was a clear impediment, then he *is* no husband. You must move on."

"But how?" Mary wailed. "What should I do?"

"We will go to Father Prior and ask his advice about how to proceed. In the meantime, Elizabeth and I will speak to Master Bartholomew and tell him we will pursue this matter. We will suggest he leaves for his own lands from whence he came. He has been a leaching fungus here at our manor for too long, enjoying our wines, hunting our deer, eating our food."

Elizabeth smiled up at Rogier, pleased that he was taking such a firm stance. Here was a more mature side to him that she welcomed.

"Do you agree as I have suggested?" Rogier's voice was deep and full of resolve. "I must have your agreement before I proceed."

When Mary spoke it was in a hoarse whisper. "I'm frightened of what he might do before he leaves."

"You will sleep in my room, with me, Mother," Elizabeth said firmly. "After he has gone we will discuss what happens next."

"And if he refuses to go?"

"He will not dare do that when I explain that he risks excommunication for his deceit with the Church." Rogier's expression was grim.

Elizabeth raised her eyebrows in an unspoken question. Her brother shrugged.

"Do you agree, Mother?" he asked.

Mary nodded.

Elizabeth kissed her mother's cheek and stood to leave with Rogier.

Once outside she asked him, "Excommunication? Is that a possibility?"

"I have no idea, but it should be enough to frighten Bartholomew. He may be a scheming devil but he is not as clever as he thinks. I think he will be frightened for his soul and do as we ask."

As they reached the foot of the staircase, Elizabeth stood on her toes to give Rogier a fleeting kiss on his cheek.

"Elizabeth! There is no need for such a display. Really!" He was her little brother again with all his childhood exasperation of having an older sister to tease him.

"Go to Folkingham and prepare your soul in the castle chapel, and I shall find Gabriel and give him the letters to release Master Pullen. I shall see you for your dubbing."

Having retrieved the missive, Elizabeth crossed the courtyard with a considerably lighter step than before, in search of Gabriel. Tomorrow he would ride to the town to gain Master Pullen's freedom and all would be well.

"Good day to you." She waved across to the farrier in his blackened leather apron as she strode towards the stables. "Such a beautiful afternoon." She smiled at the milkmaid who carried two pails from the goats tethered on the far wall. "Have you seen our bailiff?" She was content to search the manor herself and spend an hour in the balmy air.

Then she found Gabriel. He was sitting on the bank of the moat — with Avice.

The maidservant had woven a chain of daisies into a circlet and was trying to place it on Gabriel's head. She was laughing as he pulled away. "I crown thee Sir..." She trailed off when she realised Elizabeth was approaching and leapt to her feet. "Begging your pardon, my lady," she said. "I meant no disrespect. 'Twas but a game. It's such a fine day and we have an hour to spare before I must return to the kitchen to help Cook."

Elizabeth forced a smile. *Why should Gabriel not enjoy the company of this young woman? He has no other ties. It's just I've seen the way she looks at him...*

"I beg your pardon, my lady," Gabriel said. "Did you want me for some task?"

If I cannot have him, then I don't want him to go to another either. But that's not fair...

"My lady? Elizabeth?"

She came to her senses. "I'm sorry to interrupt your fun. I wanted to give you this." She held out the letter. "It is to take with you tomorrow when you ride to Burgh St Peter. The prison cells are next to the great oak doors which lead to the abbey precincts, at the far end of the market square. If you bang on the door, there will be someone there to direct you, and you must present it."

"I know it. I have only been to there once or twice and not for many years, but have no fear, I shall find Master Pullen, secure his release, and bring him home."

"Thank you."

"We shall need to stay overnight. It's twenty miles or more and it will take five or six hours at least. Perhaps at Northborough. There is a cheap hostelry there." He paused. "With two on the horse for the return it will take longer."

"Of course. Let me know when you return."

Elizabeth turned away but felt his eyes pierce her back and couldn't resist turning again. She was correct. Gabriel was watching her intently. Avice watched his expression, too. Then the maid bent to retrieve her basket from the grass behind her, and as she did so Gabriel pressed two fingers to his lips and held them to his cheek as he watched Elizabeth depart. Such a simple act left her with a thousand mixed emotions.

CHAPTER 19

It was the day of Rogier's dubbing into knighthood and he had spent the hours of darkness in the chapel at the castle, praying for his soul and for strength in service. He told Elizabeth his weapons would be laid upon the altar before him. Alaric and one other stood watch behind him, but it wasn't a place or a moment for a woman. At daybreak he would cleanse his whole body to wash away all sin before being dressed in the white clothes of purity and the red cloak representing the blood of Christ. His hose and shoes must be black to symbolise his willingness to die for any cause of his noble master.

With Gabriel having left the manor estates to ride to Burgh St Peter, Elizabeth was restless and unusually anxious. She was in the manor without those to whom she was closest. It was not the first time, but she felt oddly vulnerable. Mary had insisted she would not share Elizabeth's chamber and was with Bartholomew, but Elizabeth had heard none of the horrifying noises that had become commonplace. In fact, recently there had been little of that. She hoped he had not taken his favours elsewhere.

Elizabeth roused from the remnants of fitful sleep when there was knock at her door. Avice entered the bedchamber and pulled the waxed linen that covered the windows to one side. She watched the young woman as she moved effortlessly around the chamber and envied her position. If Gabriel were to take the maidservant for his wife, how would she, Elizabeth, ever cope? She would endure because she must.

"It's a fine day for the ceremony," Avice said. "I can only imagine the finery and the celebration to follow. You must be so excited for Sir Rogier, my lady."

Elizabeth could not contain her yawn but it gave her time to school her face and her thoughts.

The maid helped with her toilette and Elizabeth dressed with care. One of the newer gowns she'd had for her first visit to the Royal Court suited her well and cheered her spirits. She chose a fine linen cloth to bind her hair and simple jewellery to accompany her clothing. Together they packed a small travelling box for she would stay overnight at Folkingham and enjoy the festivities after the ceremony.

Mary was reluctant about coming to the castle but Bartholomew insisted. Even then she had suggested she return home after the service and not attend the after-party, but again he had been emphatic. "You will not deny me this opportunity, Wife. Lord John will be there and who knows what preferments I may be offered."

"Yes, Husband." She had given him his way with head down.

Elizabeth knew Bartholomew would relish being in stately company. Perhaps he *should* enjoy the occasion, Elizabeth thought with some glee, for this would be his last. On the morrow Rogier would return to the manor and the two of them would settle his account.

The grounds outside the chapel were crowded with workers who had received a day off from their labours to celebrate the lord of the manor becoming formerly recognised as a knight of the realm. As the weather was fair, tables were prepared in the outer bailey, laden with free food from Lord John, and a barrel of ale was waiting. Elizabeth nodded and greeted all those she knew by name. They in turn gave her their blessings and wished more for her brother, who was becoming well-liked and respected as a fair-minded and supportive overlord.

Inside, the castle chapel was crowded with local landowners and those who were already knighted from the surrounding areas. This was an important event and well attended, for here was to be another to swell their ranks when called to battle, as surely they would be soon. John of Gaunt was already on the Scottish borders and the war with France, though quieter in recent months, still rumbled on.

More, there was trouble brewing closer to home, if what Elizabeth had heard was true, and the populace were rebelling against their working conditions imposed by the landlords. Even on their own manor lands there were increased rumblings of discontent and when riders came by with pennants and loud voices about what was happening close by in other counties, it only stirred up further restlessness.

Since the early crusades the core tenets of the chivalric code had been clear: unwavering loyalty, social fellowship, and religious duty. The knight's primary occupation, however, was the call to arms. Count Ludovico, in Baldassare's *Book of the Courtier,* gave instructions that could not be ignored. If their serfs chose to disobey their lords, then there would be consequences that could be bloody.

As Elizabeth took her seat in the front row, she forgot about the local stirrings and the battles across the sea. She watched the proceedings with fervent concentration. Father Prior from Vaudey Abbey knelt before the altar dressed in his finest. His all-enveloping alb was of purest white. The chasuble over his shoulders was ornamented in red and gold and his hand-woven stole depicted religious and temporal images. His part in the ceremony would be to bless the items before handing them to Lord John. As premier knight and Lord Gaunt's representative,

Lord John, accompanied by his own knights, would witness this accolade for Rogier. Elizabeth had never been more proud of her brother than she was now.

Rogier's two sponsors stood either side of him. Alaric and another held the spurs and his sword, which Father Prior had blessed. Rogier's voice rang out with the ancient words of fealty. "I swear to defend to my utmost, the weak, the orphans, the widows, and the oppressed; I shall be courteous and all women shall receive my special care." The sponsors passed his sword to Lord John, before kneeling in homage and to fasten Rogier's new spurs to his heels.

The height of the ceremony was the dubbing, when Lord John fastened Rogier's own sword around his waist. He then touched his cheek with the flat of his own blade before allowing it to rest lightly upon each shoulder. This act, known as the *colée*, was the only time Rogier was to allow a sword upon him without fighting back.

"Be thou a knight." Lord John's deep voice rose up to the ceiling of the small chapel and Elizabeth's eyes welled. As she knelt in prayer for her brother, one tear rolled down her cheek before she wiped it away.

The feast that followed was elegant but vast, with the assembled nobility partaking of swan, peacock and salted eels, as well as various sweet desserts and plenty of fine wine to wash it all down. Minstrels played well into the night. There might have been a tournament the next day for the knights to demonstrate their skills of horsemanship and armaments, but the mounting trouble with the peasants in the south-eastern counties was calling many to attend their king in London. On this occasion Rogier was not to go with Lord John, but Alaric was.

Elizabeth returned to the manor the next day as planned, where she and Rogier would speak with Sir Bartholomew and present him with their findings about his marriage to Mary. She wasn't frightened by the prospect, but nervous anticipation engulfed her as the wooden wheels of the cart rumbled over the rough road. She had not seen Alaric that morning. He had slept in his own chamber at the castle and left with Lord John at first light. As it turned out, Rogier had gathered his things early, too, and left a message that he would see her at home.

Her thoughts rumbled on with the turn of the wheels. Gabriel should have arrived in Burgh St Peter by now. Elizabeth prayed he would find and release Master Pullen without mishap. The two would make the return journey together and after a further stopover they would be home. Elizabeth would be overjoyed to see Gabriel ride in with the sokeman.

There was a simple truth. She loved him. This was not a lightning revelation, she realised. It had been growing over the years. She had known him nearly all her life, from childhood playmate to friend, to steadfast supporter of her work at the manor to ... to what? He could never be her partner, her lover, for she was married to another and even should that not be so, the difference in their rank was unacceptable to all those around them, both nobility and commoner. *Yet*, she thought, *what of John of Gaunt, Duke of Lancaster and our patron? Has he not taken Mistress Swynford as his lover and has she not borne him children? She is significantly beneath him in status. Her husband died before they became lovers, but still, he is married.*

Elizabeth huffed and the carter turned to see if she was all right.

"Yes, yes," she said in response to his query. "I have much on my mind. Forgive me."

He smiled, revealing gaps in his teeth, and nodded his understanding.

How frustrating it is not to be able to take the lead in such a matter of the heart, as others of the higher nobility do, and also because I am a woman! It's all well for John of Gaunt to do as he pleases.

In her mind's eye she saw Gabriel striding across the bridge to greet her. His broad-shouldered physique made stronger by manual work, his dark hair, his sparkling eyes. She thought of his nimble brain from which she gained excitement as they bounced ideas back and forth and sparred with each other. She tried to dismiss these thoughts and place Alaric there instead.

Oh, but it was Gabriel she loved. And he was not here. She ached for his return.

Elizabeth was brought back to the moment by the sound of raised voices as they approached the manor. An argument was developing between a group of men and Marcus the reeve. She huffed again. This was her reality and she must accept it. The conversation stopped as she approached and they all bowed their heads to acknowledge her passing.

"Wait, please," she commanded the carter. "What have we here, Master Smith?"

"These men are refusing to work to my instructions, my lady. They have heard of insurrection in the counties of Kent and Essex where a band of men are said to be marching on London."

"My lady," one of the men addressed Elizabeth, "you and Sir Rogier have always been good to us but we cannot continue in this way. We cannot feed our families. If we could have more land — and there is land to spare after so many perished during the Great Mortality — we could produce more food. We should be able to own our own land, with respect, my lady," he added, ignoring the black look on the reeve's face.

"How dare you speak thus to her ladyship," barked Marcus. "You are insolent and ungrateful."

"This is not the place or time to discuss this," Elizabeth said directly to the men, "but I shall listen to what you have to say. Approach me at the end of the day, after vespers, and I shall listen, but now you must finish the task Master Smith has set for you. He is reeve and you must respect his position." Thus, she hoped to appease both Marcus and the men.

Elizabeth entered the great hall of the manor and immediately sought out Rogier. She must know if he had heard of this disquiet, both here at home and in the capital, where the king was currently residing and where her own husband had departed this morn. She knew Alaric would be riding hard with Lord John's retinue, especially if the revolt moving towards London was as strong as indicated, but it would take them two days at least to reach the capital.

She eventually found Rogier in the stables and urged him to walk with her.

"Sister," he said. "News travels fast these days, especially when it is not good."

"And now our own people are rebelling. Master Marcus is not helping with his intransigence. I expect a delegation after vespers this eve. We should listen to what they say and speak with them together, if we are to avert further discontent."

"We must also speak with Master Bartholomew."

"Let us do that now and get it over with. Suppose he refuses to leave?"

"He is a coward and such men lack moral fibre. He will fear for his soul if he thinks he will be threatened with excommunication for his sins, for they are not petty."

"I'm so pleased to have you at my side." She smiled up at Rogier. "Indeed, you are a knight and proud I am to call you so. Now let us go and call on Master Bartholomew before we have a change of heart."

They found him slouched in a chair with a half empty wine cup, but he was alone, a fact for which Elizabeth was grateful.

"Sir," Rogier said. "We would have words with you. In the parlour would be best."

"Whatever you have to say, young *sir*," Bartholomew replied, his voice laced with sarcasm, "you may speak it here. I am comfortable and do not wish to move."

"What I have to say, *sir*," Rogier echoed with equal derision, "you will not wish to be overheard." He lowered his voice menacingly. "It refers to your marriage to our mother and if you wish to preserve your soul, never mind your dignity, you would do well to come to the parlour."

Bartholomew's eyes narrowed, though he sighed with a pretence he cared little for what Rogier had said.

He may bluster, but the facts will be heard, Elizabeth thought.

Rogier closed the parlour door and indicated for Bartholomew to seat himself. "It has come to our attention that you have married our mother in haste and for your own gain. This marriage is against the laws of the land and against God since you are so closely related. This is a fact of which I am certain you are aware but chose to ignore."

"Why, you insolent young … this is whiffle-whaffle!"

"You know this to be true and the facts have been verified."

Bartholomew's shoulders slumped.

"Father Prior at the abbey here at Grimsthorpe knows of the facts and you stand in danger of excommunication should you do nothing to rectify this situation and remove yourself from a marriage that is no marriage in reality. You are nothing but a *rakefire*."

He certainly has outstayed his welcome, Elizabeth thought, trying to hide a smile.

"You have been cruel beyond words to our mother and all in the name of greed. In addition to your own lands, you thought you would have this manor, our birthright, but you were wrong, sir. As it is you have lived on our bounty all these months and taken as your own what was not. You have until midday tomorrow to be gone back from whence you came."

"But I…"

"If you are not gone then Father Prior will become involved and representation will be made to Rome. Make no mistake, this will happen."

"You cannot… I will not…"

"You will risk being shunned by all? You will risk being unable to take the holy sacrament and all that means? You will risk your soul not finding Heaven? Surely not, sir. Consider what you lose by staying. It is to be thus no longer." Rogier placed his hands on the table and leaned forward to glare at Sir Bartholomew. "You have until tomorrow!" With these words he escorted Elizabeth from the room and went in search of Mary, who they found in her private solar.

It was a tearful interview when the brother and sister told their mother that she would be safe from now on. Elizabeth called for Avice to bring a sleeping draught and when she was certain Mary was in a state of untroubled sleep, she and Rogier retired to the hall to sit by the fire and breathe a sigh of relief.

It was only a few moments, however, before Rogier cleared his throat. "Elizabeth, what of Isabelle? She should not be forced to leave the manor and return with her father, surely?"

"No, she should not, but she may wish to leave with him."

"We have not considered her position sufficiently. I blame myself. I have been thinking of Mother and my dubbing and I have not been considerate enough."

"You have been busy at the castle, Brother. Before, you suggested your emotions were heightened for Isabelle. Is that still so?"

"Yes. We have spent more time together since I have been at home, especially while you were in London. I do believe I should like to take her for my wife."

"Then why don't you go and find her now and explain all."

"She may never speak with me again when I tell her of our conversation with her father."

"I have witnessed the lack of love between father and daughter. She has been in an invidious position here, probably knowing how things were between her father and our mother. I think I have paid her too little heed as well. I am as guilty as you, Brother. I will make amends but you must find her with all speed and ensure she understands she will be welcome here should she wish to stay. She will continue to be a good companion for Mother."

With this, Rogier hurried from the fireside to find Isabelle. He turned after he had taken several paces. "Perhaps I shall ride to Folkingham after I have spoken with her and ask Lady Katherine, in Lord John's absence, if she thinks he might be agreeable to our marriage. Then, when he returns, I shall be able to speak to him with confidence."

Elizabeth nodded. "If she accepts you for a husband, I shall be certain she knows she is a true sister to me." She settled back in her chair, exhausted but awaiting vespers when the group of workers were due to plead their case.

CHAPTER 20

In the distance the abbey bells chimed the hour of vespers. The sound travelled in the still air of early evening and Elizabeth anticipated the arrival of the men who wanted to share their grievances about shortage of labour and the ownership of the spare land that currently lay fallow. To a great extent her hands were held fast by the laws of the young King Richard, but she and her people might come to an agreement. Hearing movement in the courtyard, she rose from her chair and stood by the hearth in preparation for their arrival.

When no one came, she sat again, puzzled, and when a maidservant asked if she should prepare the table for dinner, Elizabeth agreed. Perhaps the men had changed their minds. Marcus may have deterred them. She would seek him out on the morrow and ask.

With Gabriel gone to Burgh St Peter, Alaric in London, and Rogier flown to Folkingham, perhaps she would seek out Isabelle. Rogier would have spoken with her by now and she must also make her peace and ensure the young woman could feel confident if she wanted to stay. Of Bartholomew there was no sign and Mary was still sleeping. Elizabeth stood to leave the hall and seek out her stepsister when a commotion in the courtyard stayed her progress.

The huge door opened and a man stepped into the hall. The stranger looked around and, seeing Elizabeth standing by the fire, he approached with a small bow.

"Lady Elizabeth, I am Master Thomas Doughty. I have ridden hard from London." Indeed, his clothing was travel-stained and his shoes were muddy. Then she recognised him as one of Alaric's squires. "My lady, I bring news from the capital."

Seeing his serious expression, Elizabeth clasped her hands to her breast. "Is my husband well? Is he safe?"

"Oh yes, my lady. Forgive me. He sends greetings."

"Please come and be seated." She called for refreshment for the visitor. "I know you now, but you are new, are you not?"

"Yes, my lady." He was young, his unblemished skin flushed from the ride and his hair was tousled as he grabbed his cap from his head. "I have come from Sir Alaric with word of the situation as it is. He wished you to know that he is safe, should you hear rumours, for there are large crowds descending on the capital."

A maid arrived from the kitchens. On a tray was a mug of ale and some oat biscuits with goat's cheese and a dish of stewed onions. "Will the good sir be staying for dinner, my lady?"

"Yes. Please lay the table with an extra bowl. It will be for myself and Master Doughty here, only. My lady mother is resting. Master Bartholomew and Mistress Isabelle are in their rooms." Then she added, "As far as I know."

When the maid had left she turned to Master Thomas. "Please tell me all."

"There is disturbance among the populace but there is some suggestion Lord John of Gaunt has formally renounced his relationship with Lady Katherine Swynford and reconciled with his wife, Lady Constance, in the hope it would still the crowd," he said. "But it has not."

Elizabeth raised an eyebrow in surprise. "Lady Katherine Swynford is a vibrant beauty. I saw them together at court. They say he loves her dearly and showers her with gifts and that … well … that his wife is austere and not really to his taste at all."

"He must have a way to recover some popularity, but it doesn't seem to be working. Currently, a great crowd have gathered south of the river, though they don't seem too aggressive at the moment and are praising Richard as their king. They will advance, they say."

"There has been unrest for some time. Even here," Elizabeth said, thinking of the deputation from her own workers that she was set to receive. "I heard that a preacher named John Wycliffe has been talking about equality for all. Is he behind this?"

"Not really, though he gives the uprising — for that is what it has become — a moral heart. The rebel crowd already pushed their way through the gateway and into the keep at Rochester Castle and took the constable, Sir John Newington, as hostage, along with his wife and children to ensure his compliance. Another group from Essex have raided Lesnes Abbey and burned all the court rolls there."

"Why would they do that?" Elizabeth felt a stir of fear.

"The papers control the peasantry. They aim to steal as many official papers as possible and burn them as they're all records of payments and livings."

"And what of Rochester? It's a huge castle. It guards Watling Street and the River Medway."

"Perhaps the rebels had help from within, but now they have Newington's wife and children they also have a bargaining tool. Someone called Johanna Ferrour joined the rebels there with her husband, John. She's formidable, they say."

"A woman?"

"Oh yes, there are several women involved, and she, in particular, is a leader. And several of the rebels are military men with years of warfare experience. This is not a rabble of peasants at all. That's why it's becoming such a serious threat."

"What of my husband? You're sure he is safe?"

"Yes, my lady. He is within the city walls of London. The rebels entered Canterbury Cathedral and a man named Wat Tyler discovered in the papers there that the Archbishop…"

"Sir Simon of Sudbury?"

"Yes, he has vast riches and it has infuriated Master Tyler's rebels even more. Now they are heading for London, and thousands are camped on the common land outside the walls at Blackheath. It's all been coordinated and carefully planned and several churches have burned."

Elizabeth put her hand to her mouth. "They must be desperate to take such actions."

"A group took Sir John Newington and entered the Tower of London itself."

Elizabeth gasped. "Oh, my word. That's where the king is. He's only a boy."

"Nearly a man at fourteen and doing a man's work, my lady. The Constable of Rochester assured the king the rebels meant him no harm and they saw him as their rightful monarch. Your husband was told all this by Lord John Beaumont, my lady. He said that the rebels were angry about the king's uncle, John of Gaunt, and the men of the Church who have riches beyond imagination while others starve."

"Lord Gaunt believes he has a duty to preserve the crown for Richard. Lord John is the duke's man and will always support him, but I really cannot believe Gaunt is wicked enough to take the crown. He has a sense of responsibility for his nephew. After all, King Richard is the son of Edward of Woodstock, whom he worshiped; his favoured brother's son."

"Dinner is served, my lady," Avice said as she carried a tray laden with steaming food.

Elizabeth indicated for Master Doughty to join her at table.

Once seated, she said, "I hear that Lord Gaunt, the Duke of Lancaster is near Scotland. He's not in London."

"That is so and without his guidance, King Richard agreed to meet the rebels. It seems he has seized the opportunity to rule on his own."

"He is young and believes in his divine right, but there is responsibility that goes with that and he is still learning."

"King Richard went by barge along the Thames to Rotherhithe but refused to go ashore and meet the rebels. He and his men returned to London without speaking to them at all and they were much displeased."

"It must have been a shock for him and his attendants to see so many gathered there, all demanding things of him."

"Fear, too, my lady. There were thousands of malcontents there."

"What happened next?"

"The rebel crowd marched on London. No one stopped them at London Bridge. They could have raised the drawbridge in the middle, but we believe the commoners of the city have sympathy for the rebels. That is when Sir Alaric bade me come to you."

Elizabeth was troubled. Never had she heard of such a thing before, and their lives were being disrupted in an attempt to overturn the natural order. Oh, how she wished Gabriel was nearby with his good sense, loyalty and understanding. Yet her people had not come to see her as she anticipated. In this she took some comfort. Perhaps they realised that everything would work out.

Thomas Doughty departed the next morning at sunup. He had a long ride ahead of him. Elizabeth anticipated Rogier's return and she hoped Sir Bartholomew would depart, although she had not seen him and was thus spared any further unpleasantness. She would find Marcus and enquire of him about the atmosphere among the villeins and reassure herself that he had not prevented them from coming to see her.

Avice brought her morning milk and drew back the linens. "Good morning, my lady. It's a fine morn, but I am worried." She frowned and looked pale.

"What is it, Avice?" Elizabeth's immediate thoughts were of discontent and workers marching upon the manor. She sat up.

"It's Master Gabriel. Surely he should have returned by now?"

Elizabeth thought for a moment. There seemed no doubt that Avice had a fancy for Gabriel. "Possibly," she replied, "but it may have taken him a little longer than he thought to find the right person to free Master Pullen. Then the journey home will be slow. He talked of an overnight stop since they would not be riding at speed and the horse will need to rest, with transporting two." The more she spoke, the more she realised she was trying to convince herself. Avice's words had awoken a gnawing anxiety.

Elizabeth arose with speed and dressed, determined to seek out Isabelle before going to find Marcus.

The young woman was sitting in the orchard, under the boughs. The sun was weak but there was no wind and it was mild. She must have been collecting the roots from the madder in the hedgerows for her light shawl was a dark crimson. She was gazing into the distance and was startled by Elizabeth's approach.

"Do not fear," Elizabeth smiled her reassurance. "I only wish to say that you have become as a sister to me and I hope you will stay with us. I presume Rogier spoke with you yester eve?"

"Yes, he did. He explained all regarding my father and our situation here. Your brother is always so gentle and kind to me. Unlike my parent," she added with a frown. "I have been worrying what will become of me. I do not wish to return to our own village. My life before we arrived here was desolate."

"My mother will continue to welcome your company should you remain with us. I, too," Elizabeth added.

Isabelle looked at her as silent tears ran down her cheeks. Since Elizabeth had been at court and seen King Richard carry something he called a handkerchief, she had done the same and passed her new sister the square of soft linen to dab her eyes. "Have you seen your father this morning?"

"Not to speak with, but I saw him in the distance." She pointed across the fields on the other side of the moat. "He was talking to a group of men. I recognised Master Martin but it was too far away to be certain who else was there and, of course, I could hear nothing."

A shiver of unease ran through Elizabeth. Bartholomew could wreak untold disruption before he left, should he choose, and she doubted not he would take pleasure in so doing. "Please consider staying here, Isabelle. Rogier should return from Folkingham this morning and he will say the same. Now, I must hurry to find the reeve."

Before she could do so, however, there was the clatter of an arrival over the wooden bridge across the moat, and she hurried to see who it might be, praying it would be Gabriel but knowing from the speed of approach and the sound of the hooves that it could not possibly be he. It was her brother, but coming at such a speed she wondered why. He entered the courtyard and threw himself from the saddle.

Elizabeth ran to him. "Why the haste?"

"I have been ordered to Scotland with all speed. Since Lord John and several of his knights are protecting the king in London, the Duke of Lancaster wishes the rest of us to join him until other arrangements are made. Is that not exciting, Sister? I shall be riding as a knight for the first time, with my own squires and maybe even into battle."

Elizabeth's stomach sank. This was not what she needed at this time of unrest and uncertainty.

"I must fine Isabelle, first. Where is she?"

"In the orchard. I have spoken with her about staying here."

Rogier turned away but she took his arm before he could leave. "What of the problems here? The workers' unrest and Sir Bartholomew?"

"Elizabeth, I would stay if I could, but I have an order and I must serve my liege lord. You know this. You are capable of overseeing things here. More so than I, truth be told."

She sighed. "Of course. Find Isabelle and reassure her of her position. When you return from the north we shall have a wedding feast, no doubt."

"We shall." Rogier grinned and ran off towards the orchard.

Elizabeth smiled. One moment a man; the next, still a youth.

Then he turned. "Before I leave I shall tell you what I learned at the castle. A messenger arrived with news for Katherine and she told me of events in London."

Elizabeth thought she had already heard of what he spoke. Was there more?

She went in search of the reeve.

Marcus was emphatic he had not deterred the men from speaking to her. "My lady, I would not be so underhand," he said.

Elizabeth watched him closely, wondering if he spoke the truth. His face held no subterfuge and his eyes fixed directly upon her.

"In fact, I've seen none of them this morning. I was going to ask them how they fared in the meadow with the thistles. They are particularly bad at the moment and we want none going to seed or it will be a thousand times worse next year. I shall visit the village and enquire of them, my lady, but first I must check on one of the ploughs. It has a cracked mouldboard, I am told."

"Very well, Master Reeve. Thank you for that."

Elizabeth's next stop was the stables but as she walked, she thought hard about all she had learned. Bartholmew had spoken with some men in the field. Marcus had not seen hide nor hair of that group. Something was amiss here.

At the stables, the lad told her that Master Bartholomew had wanted a horse. "He had a cloth sack as well as a leather bag with him and so requested a rouncey, saying his things were heavy and he needed a mount that could manage that."

"What time did he say he would return?" she asked.

"He didn't, my lady. He said he was going out and may be some time, but he didn't say where he was going or for how long."

"Thank you," Elizabeth said and returned to the hall to await Rogier.

When he returned, Isabelle was on his arm. She smiled her greetings to Elizabeth and hurried to embrace her. "Are you aware of what Rogier has asked me? He has spoken to Lady Katherine at Folkingham. I could not be happier. Of course, he must obtain Lord John's agreement and that won't be for some time because of the troubles in London. My goodness they sound…" She would have said more but Rogier put his hand on her arm to ensure she drew breath.

"Let me tell Elizabeth the latest news from the capital," he said in gentle tones.

Isabelle bowed her head. "Pardon my excitement. Yes. In London, it is truly terrible."

"A messenger arrived with news from Alaric, so I know of what you speak," Elizabeth said.

"Have you heard about the Tower?"

"The Tower of London? What has happened there?"

"The members of the uprising poured through all the houses on London Bridge and crossed the Thames, ransacking the offices and homes of lawyers. Everywhere they go they are burning papers. They went wild after the king left without speaking to them at Rotherhithe."

"Why wasn't the drawbridge in the middle of London Bridge raised to prevent them? Surely that was the point at which they could easily have been stopped?"

"Perhaps they had help from the common folk? Apparently the rebels were welcomed. I suppose they are seen as not so different to those who dwell within and beyond the city walls. That's not the worst, though, Sister."

Elizabeth's eyes widened and Isabelle, who had already heard all, wrapped her arms around her as if in protection.

"They moved on to the home of our own Duke of Lancaster at the Savoy Palace."

"John of Gaunt's home is full of the most fabulous riches. That would anger them further, I suppose. He's already unpopular."

"They have burnt it to the ground and were told to ignore the wealth inside. I'm not sure they have all done that. The ringleader is a woman! Can you believe that?"

"Yes, Master Doughty mentioned her name when he was here — Johanna Ferrour, I believe."

"Some of the rebels got trapped in the wine cellar of the Savoy and their screams could be heard for days, but not her."

Elizabeth shuddered at the thought.

"She stole a chest of coins and shared them among some friends, keeping some for herself."

"It must have been a great temptation, even if they said they weren't after riches but wanted a change in the order of things."

"Yes. The leaders were trying to quell the violence but it became impossible."

"I can imagine. It sounds like the people are enraged. The latest poll tax has been the last straw."

"I cannot listen a second time, it's too frightening," said Isabelle. "I shall go to the kitchen and ask for refreshments."

Rogier turned to Elizabeth. "That's as much as I have been told. Lady Katherine didn't know any more. I must prepare to ride out from Folkingham with the rest of the company, so must pack a chest and be gone."

"I hope the unrest doesn't spread up here. I'm a little worried about some of our serfs. They are restless. We have done our best to ensure fairness, but is that enough?"

"Gabriel will be here soon. It sounds as if Sir Bartholomew has taken our advice and left. I asked at the stables on my way in here. Isabelle is relieved, I can tell you. I'm sorry, Sister, but I must leave."

"I understand. I'll seek out Isabelle. Together we shall be fine. Please look after yourself and come back to us in safety, dear Brother, for you are indeed dear to us all."

CHAPTER 21

News spread by word of mouth with speed and just as well, for matters were moving with haste. A passing traveller who asked for alms at Vaudey Abbey brought the latest information and Elizabeth heard of it when one of the monks came to the manor. He was a young man, the hem of his habit stained from walking through fields and along the lanes. His hair was unclipped, demonstrating he was yet to be ordained.

"On the 13th of June they fired the premises of the Knights Hospitaller in Clerkenwell. It's outrageous! The Order is an international power above the nobility and answers directly to the Pope."

Elizabeth was thoughtful. "They give succour to the poor and the sick and are a healing brotherhood." She paused. She was of the nobility and had been taught to believe in the structure of their society, and yet... "They own much land and have great wealth. Perhaps this seems unfair to those who have so little."

"Some man named Thomas Farndon has encouraged others to set fires and steal goods," the monk continued. "There is also talk of ... of beheadings, my lady."

Elizabeth was shocked. "The ordinary people are suffering greatly and when they see riches such as the nobility and the Church have, they must find it almost impossible to understand or tolerate," she said. "But that doesn't excuse such violence. Perhaps they see no other way, though it's hard to know the truth of it all, Father. We try hard here at the manor to be benevolent."

"They broke into Newgate and freed all the criminals," the monk continued, shaking his head.

Elizabeth could hardly believe it either and imagined plumes of smoke across the city she had so recently visited and by which she had been charmed. She had seen areas of vast wealth as well as people looking impoverished, but it had always been thus. Any landowner, if they had a grain of sense and compassion, would ensure the poorest were supported and not abandoned. That was how things worked. That is how society replenished and progressed. She was stirred from her reverie by the monk's voice.

"There's a place called Mile End, being one mile from the Aldgate. King Richard agreed to meet a deputation there. One of the leaders, a man named Wat Tyler, demanded an end to serfdom in England. He claims that no person should work for another without a regular and fair covenant."

"This is what the preacher John Ball is saying, that all men should be equal and no one should pay homage to another but should receive payment that is equitable."

"Yes my lady, but —" he cleared his throat — "John Ball does not speak as a recognised voice of religion."

"No, of course not." She was suitably chastised by the young monk and moved hastily on to safer ground. "It is very brave of the king to speak with his people like that, especially when they are clearly so angered."

"He had his nobles and knights with him."

Elizabeth wondered if Alaric had been there.

The monk continued, "This man Tyler said he trusted King Richard and believed in his good grace, but asked that all those around the king who serve him with evil intent should be arrested and tried for treason."

Elizabeth gasped. "Treason? They surely cannot mean John of Gaunt. He may make mistakes but he is sincere in his service to Richard as king, surely? Would Sir Alaric have been there? I expect Lord John would."

"Quite probably, my lady. Anyway, it is said King Richard agreed to all this, and when the rebel crowd asked that all commoners should be in bond no more, he agreed to that too."

Elizabeth was puzzled. "How will it work? What must we do here?"

"Yes, well…" The monk turned and paced, rubbing his hand over his hair and leaving it tousled like a child's fresh from sleep. "I sense these promises have not gone forward. I believe that the knights accompanying the king wanted rid of these people and then they could be left to sort it out, so they were happy he agreed to anything," he said before adding, "and the king is young and inexperienced."

Elizabeth sighed. "Perhaps old enough to be proud of himself for making his first major decision on his own, but without realising the consequences. I mean, how can we adopt all those demands here? It's not realistic."

"But that was not the end. While the king was out, another force entered the Tower of London. They found Sir Simon of Sudbury in the chapel there."

"Thomas Doughty told me when they broke into Canterbury, the rebel crowd were livid about the riches he had accumulated as Archbishop."

"Yes, and I'm sorry to tell you that they have murdered him. It was a messy death, apparently."

Elizabeth was horrified afresh. "He only recently resigned as the king's chancellor, but it was he who was responsible for implementing the last poll tax."

"They also seized Robert Hales. He was the king's Lord High Treasurer and also incredibly wealthy."

"Was?"

"They put him to the sword, too. He has met his maker, we hope." He made the sign of the cross.

"What of John of Gaunt's son and heir — Henry Bolingbroke? We met him at Folkingham. Near neighbours almost. He must have been in the Tower. I heard he had ridden to London in his father's absence." Knowing how unpopular John of Gaunt had become, Elizabeth feared the worst for him.

"One of the rebels' leaders, Johanna Ferrour, and her husband John, hid him in a cupboard when the rebels were rampaging through the Tower."

Elizabeth found a smile. "Praise the Lord." It was a small relief in this story of blood and mayhem.

"Chaos continued and there was another meeting with the king at a place called Smithfield. Our monarch asked why the people had not dispersed and gone home. Wat Tyler stepped forward again, and this time demanded more. He wanted less power and reform of the Church. It seems the list on the petition grows outrageous." The young monk's voice rose in his indignation at the suggestion that the Church was at fault. "There was a fracas. I'm not sure how it happened but the Mayor of London stabbed Wat Tyler and another nobleman ran him through with a sword."

Elizabeth sighed deeply. She prayed that the nobleman was not Lord John or, worse, her own husband. No good ever came of rebellion in the face of unequal arms, even if the cause was just. This thought surprised her. She was beginning to see the cause was perhaps one of moral reasoning.

"The king shouted out 'You shall have no captain but me. I am your king. Be all in rest and peace'. The traveller who told us this shouted out those words, just as the king had done. I understand the crowd dispersed at this point and the nobles are saying all is over but that's not the truth. There are riots elsewhere, we have heard, as far away as Somerset and Devon in the west, and York and Scarborough in the north."

"So it's far from over?"

"I fear that is so, my lady. Norwich is having problems. A man named Geoffrey Lister is stirring trouble and calling men to arms. He even called himself the 'king of the county commoners'. There has been burning of papers and … and churches, as there has been recently in London."

"It seems particularly foolhardy to call himself such a name as 'king of the county'. Norwich is such a wealthy city. The ordinary people will be easily riled into an attack in the current climate."

"The second city in the land, my lady. Perhaps I should not say this but Bishop Henry Despenser there is a determined man with a background of war in Italy, as well as taking his current position from the Pope himself. He will stand no dissent at all." His voice lowered to almost a whisper. "They do say his sermons are fierce and people have accused him of lacking compassion."

"He is brutal, you mean, and does not listen to reason."

The monk bowed his head. "Father Prior was overheard to say as much, but I cannot speak thus. I've heard they call Despenser the Fighting Bishop. He, along with a company of knights, have just slain a deposition of the common people who were on their way to see the king, but it's not for me to pass judgement on my betters."

It was Elizabeth's turn to turn and pace. This was all so worrying, and this young monk had just admitted to believing Bishop Despenser to be his 'better' when he had murdered a deputation of working people.

"My lady, may I speak plainly?"

"I would hope you will," she said.

"I said just now that the riots are spreading, west and north. Well, I have heard that such a riot is planned for Burgh St Peter, within our own diocese. Some of the local men are gathering. What if Bishop Despenser is called upon to aid our own monks at the Abbey of St Peter, as I have heard is possible? We have no men involved in this, have we?"

Elizabeth gasped. "I don't know. Will you excuse me, Father? Thank you for bringing me this information. I must verify the safety of our people."

"Of course. Go in peace." He gave her his hurried blessing before turning to leave.

Elizabeth needed time and space to consider all she had learned. Gabriel was still away in Burgh St Peter, the very place under threat of riot and danger. Were some of her own people missing, or were they simply busy working in a remote part of the manor lands? Bartholomew had been seen having a heated conversation with a group of men. She would not put it past him to have stirred up trouble as his parting shot before disappearing. He would take revenge if he could, of that she was certain. She must seek out Marcus and ask him where they were.

Elizabeth was riding a pony towards the fields when she saw Marcus coming towards her, almost at a run. He was quite out of breath and as he reached her he bent forward, placing his hands on his knees and puffing. "Forgive me, Lady Elizabeth," he said. "I have news." He straightened and then bowed his head in proper fashion.

"Master Reeve. I was looking for you."

"If I may speak first, my lady? My words are of foremost importance."

She inclined her head in acknowledgement of his request and at that moment she saw a flash of his younger brother. The same colouring, of course, but also a certain expression, undefined but there nonetheless. It gave her a jolt of yearning for Gabriel and she clasped a fist to her chest with a sudden irrational fear for him.

"Are you all right?" Marcus asked. "You look pale."

Elizabeth took a breath and straightened her back. "Yes. Please tell me what you have heard, I'm so concerned for our workers at the moment."

"I believe Master Martin and his friends have gone to Burgh St Peter. Sir Bartholomew was seen speaking with the same group not an hour before and Master Durand, who has remained here, told me he was stirring trouble —" He broke off. "Forgive me, Lady Elizabeth, for speaking ill of your stepfather. I meant nothing by it. I ..."

"Do not concern yourself," she said. "I understand." She hurried on, "I need to know what was said."

"Sir Bartholomew was encouraging their unrest. He spoke to them of the little they have, and all they should have. He told them they do all the hard, back-breaking work but, forgive me, mistress, it's the noblemen and women who receive all the rewards. Sir Bartholomew thought I would ally myself with him. I could not. You have been good to me here and I do not want to lose my position." Elizabeth saw the earnest expression on his face and believed him. "I haven't always been as supportive as I should, and for that I apologise, my lady. I was envious of

Gabriel when there was no need. I understand how he feels about you — and his position here," he added in haste. "He respects his position, but he... Oh, my lady, I must say this. He loves you and ... and he is loyal and trustworthy and I wish to be more like him." Marcus rushed through this last sentence in his embarrassment, and a warmth rushed through Elizabeth.

For several seconds she was speechless and then she gathered herself. "Thank you, Marcus. Where is Sir Bartholomew now?"

"He has ridden out, my lady. At the stables they wondered if he would return." He frowned. "If you are going to seek these troublemakers I should accompany you, mistress, and bring these good-for-nothings back."

"No, Marcus. I shall see to that. But they are not 'good-for-nothing'. These are momentous times and perhaps we all need to review our place in it."

With that, they took leave of each other and Elizabeth returned to the manor.

She must decide the best course of action. The men from the manor were on their way to Burgh St Peter to do God only knew what and it was highly likely they would up on the wrong end of a lance if Bishop Despenser was truly involved.

But she was the wife of a nobleman, a knight of the realm, and Lord John was a right-hand man of the king himself, placed highly at court and well respected. It was clear which side of this debate they would land. She wasn't frightened of travelling such a distance alone. She could don Rogier's clothing and be taken for a young squire. She had done similar before, though this time she would bundle a dress into a bag and take it with her. She wouldn't want to be accused of improper dress and risk imprisonment herself.

Isabelle would need to be told of her plan so she might weave an appropriate story should it become necessary. Burgh St Peter was no more than seven leagues away and she would be riding fast in the hope of overtaking the men from the manor, who were on foot. Then, hopefully, they would follow her home before trouble overtook them all. Perhaps she might meet Gabriel with Master Pullen on the road, too.

A courser might be the better ride. It was a significantly stronger and larger horse that one she might normally choose, but suited to a long journey and the persona of a young man. The weather was set fair and she planned to spend a few hours resting in woodland near Northborough. Elizabeth went to the kitchen to forage for bread, cheese and a small flagon of ale. She took some apples from the storeroom. It would be enough to give her sustenance along the way.

It was past noon when Elizabeth, dressed in Rogier's clothing, set off over the bridge across the moat and along the track towards the main route. She had opted for a gipon Rogier had outgrown, which fitted her well and had the advantage of a padded front, which disguised her womanly shape. A long hood would disguise her chestnut locks all the better. Although Rogier's cotehardie was more fitted, the sleeves were decorated, displaying the Amundeville family coat of arms, which she would employ should it become necessary.

She could see a long way ahead, the road being an old Roman route and very straight. After a hard ride she was almost halfway and approaching Northborough. The manor house there was comparatively new, only forty years old and built by Roger de Northborough, Bishop of Lichfield. While she had heard talk of him, Elizabeth barely knew the people there, and rather than explain her mission and the reasons for dressing as she was, she stopped for the night in woodland and settled to rest, allow the horse to graze on the grass among the trees.

Daybreak was early at this time of year and before full light the bird song stirred her uneasy sleep. The piercing trill of a robin followed by the more melodious blackbird made her open her eyes and by the time the sparrows and finches had joined the chorus she was fully awake. She would find a field pond for her mount to refresh himself and to splash her own face, and she would recommence her journey.

By the time Elizabeth approached the walls of Burgh St Peter she was beginning to think her mission was a hopeless one. She had expected to overtake her workers since she had followed the obvious route but there had been no sign of them. Nor had there been any sign of Gabriel, and she prayed for his safety.

CHAPTER 22

As Elizabeth approached Town Bridge she drew her horse to a halt and paid the toll. She crossed over the River Nene and stopped on the other side, glancing around. It was a busy area of wharves. Ships were being loaded with much clanking and thumping of goods being hauled, and men shouting. The river was tidal. It was a major route for goods from the centre of England. From here they might go north to the Hanseatic League warehouses at Bishop's Lynn, or to Boston and thereafter to the Low Countries. Between these centres of commerce, riches could be made aplenty.

The great abbey bells started to chime, unexpectedly, for it was not one of the hours of the day. The sound of voices ahead grew louder, drawing her forwards, and she started the ride up Hythegate, a narrow street little more than twenty feet across and with few places to hide should it become necessary. The street was busy and numerous feet and hooves raised dust clouds, for it led from the quayside to the centre of the town. Elizabeth stopped a man with a loaded sack on his back and asked why the bells were ringing.

"Young sir," he said politely, touching his cap. "There's trouble afoot to be sure. Men are gathering up yonder in the market square." He turned and pointed behind him. "They're angry and many are armed."

Elizabeth lowered her voice and hid her chin in her clothing. "Is this in support of rebellious troubles elsewhere?"

"Aye, London, Norfolk, and the rest. I heard north of here, too, somewhere called Derby and again in Yorkshire." His eyes darted around fearfully. She let him go and he hurried away.

Elizabeth continued towards the market. She knew where she was now. Straight ahead of her ran Long Causeway, almost an extension of the street along which she rode but wider and clearly used as an overspill from the main market area. To her right was the great oak portal to the Abbey of St Peter with its rooms above, but the massive door was closed and the bells were loud, as if announcing to all that trouble was coming. The monks here were not risking being ransacked, as those churches and palaces elsewhere had been. Elizabeth imagined them scurrying around inside, hurriedly hiding precious papers and records. The abbey prison was to the left of the main gate and she sent a silent prayer that Gabriel had rescued Master Pullen, for surely any rabble would try to break in there as in towns elsewhere. To her left was a covered building that was the butter market. Cowgate and the butcheries lay beyond, and Elizabeth thought she caught the faint smell of blood on the breeze.

Stopping another man, she pointed to a building opposite the abbey and asked, "Is that the infirmary?"

"Aye, the Infirmary of Saint Thomas the Martyr. Have you come to pray at the holy relics in the abbey? It is not a good time, if I may be so bold. The abbey will have St Oswald's right arm and the blood of St Thomas of Canterbury under firm guard. I doubt you'll even get in. It'll be like a fortress by now. Running scared they are and I shall be too at any minute. I heard Bishop Despenser is heading this way."

"The Fighting Bishop?"

"The very same. I heard the helm fits more comfortably on his brow than the mitre. I wouldn't stay here, sir. He's been tying up his brother's business at Burley-on-the-Hill, near Oakham, only two or three hours' ride away. No doubt he'll be here imminently."

A rhythmic beating and chanting began. It seemed to be advancing and the man nodded at her before rushing away. Elizabeth dismounted and, not daring to leave her valuable animal, led the horse by the reins. She walked with caution towards the sound. What she saw caused her heart to thump in her chest.

A great press of men was approaching. Many wore padded jackets and some had mail coats, clearly expecting trouble. Some had wrapped their heads in rope for protection. Some carried hand axes while others carried field tools which had been modified, including billhooks with lethal spikes added to the top and back. Some had flails they would normally use for threshing during the harvest — spikes had been added to these too. They were heavy and could easily maim and kill their own as well as the enemy as they were swung. Elizabeth was horrified and determined to find her own workers before they became fully involved in something they would regret, or even risk losing their own lives.

She must hazard leaving the horse and found a hitching ring against the infirmary wall. She peered around the corner. It wasn't long before she saw Master Martin next to Master Bernard marching with grim expressions.

There was nothing else for it. She lowered her voice and called their names. The noise all around was raucous and the abbey bells added a thunderous quality to the air. They didn't respond. She must risk using her normal voice above the cacophony.

Master Martin turned and scanned as she called his name again. She saw him nudge his companion and nod in her direction. Both men left the horde and came towards her and then she saw Master Richard heading her way, too.

"Mistress, you shouldn't be here." His expression was one of alarm.

"And neither should you. There is an armed force approaching and none will be spared. We must leave. Are there any other of our workers?"

"Master Boucher came with us but we got separated," said Master Martin.

"You'll be killed if you stay. There will be no pity and no one will hear your pleas. Return with me now and I shall listen to your grievances, I promise."

"This is a just cause, my lady," Master Bernard said.

At that moment Master Boucher joined them. Elizabeth saw him do a double-take, having caught sight of his comrades as he marched past. "Master de Ath told us we should fight for our rights. We wish you no harm, mistress, but he said there is nothing you can do. If we return, it will be to the same thing. Our families will starve and we will have no more land than before."

"That's not true. I've said I shall listen and I shall act."

"Sorry, mistress, but I'm going on." Master Boucher turned away.

"No — come back with me!" Elizabeth shouted. "Bishop Despenser is coming. He'll have an armed force. You'll be slain!"

There was no further response from Master Boucher; he was either deaf to her pleading or determined in his stance. Elizabeth turned to the other three men. "I'm begging you, please leave with me now, before it's too late. Your families need you alive."

All three hesitated.

At that moment there was a metallic clanking in the distance. "Come!" Elizabeth shouted.

"Wait! I know you." Someone grabbed Elizabeth's wrist. It was several moments before she recognised his leer and rotten teeth.

It was the guard from Folkingham Castle. Peter Parry.

"Take your hand from me," she growled. Then, despite her contempt for him, she said, "You best leave here straight away. Bishop Despenser's men are approaching. Listen!"

Parry laughed. "Right on time, then. No doubt a bishop will be interested in why you're dressed thus." He looked her up and down.

"This way!" Master Martin shouted as the three men from the manor ran across the open area of the market and between the stalls. Elizabeth turned to see an armoured force descending on the protesters. At their fore was a knight who seemed all the larger for the full armour with helm that he wore. With sword in hand, he flailed and hacked at all he passed, man, woman or child, for whole communities had joined the protest. Behind him rode more knights dressed similarly. The screaming started. The people scattered. They were no match for the soldiers as they sliced and swung and battered the crowd. There was a piecing shriek as someone was trampled in the chaos. Panic ensued as desperate men and women tried to escape the carnage caused by the men on horseback and even more archers, who quickly encircled the people and aimed indiscriminately into the crowd.

There is no honour in this killing, Elizabeth thought. *Where is a knights code of chivalry today?*

Parry let go of Elizabeth's wrist as he turned and watched with a horror that matched her own. She took her opportunity, running to follow her men. Before disappearing up a narrow alley away from the market square, she turned and saw Parry drop to his knees, an arrow lodged in his neck and blood spurting from the wound. She turned back and ran as fast as she could from the bloody mayhem.

"We could seek sanctuary in the Chapel of St Thomas of Canterbury, just over there!" Elizabeth shouted, pointing to the entrance beside the great gate of the abbey.

"No, let's get right away!" Master Martin shouted back.

They fled down tiny back lanes and across wider roads. Past shops and houses. They didn't stop until they were far away from the uproar, although the sound of cries and clashing metal followed them.

Eventually they found themselves far enough from the town, heading towards the old watermill and into Mill Fields, where they collapsed under a hedge to catch their breath. No one said a word as each dwelt on the horror they had witnessed — and only just avoided. It had been the random slaughter of innocents and of those who only wanted a better life. After a brief rest they avoided Boroughbury Manor and headed north. They had a long walk ahead. Elizabeth would never see her horse again, and they wouldn't get home until the next day.

Elizabeth was late arising, the long trudge having been almost too much towards the end. She had refused the offer from the men to be carried, even though she didn't doubt she slowed them. Physically she was no worse for the events of the previous day, but the sights she had witnessed continue to haunt her thoughts. When she went to visit Mary to ask after her well-being, her smile felt far from genuine. Her only consolation was the thought of the three men who had returned to their families, but even that was tempered by the thought of Master Boucher probably lying dead, torn and bleeding among the wreckage of the market place they had left.

And what of Gabriel? There was still no sign of either he nor Master Pullen. If they had been caught up in the rebellion...

Finally, Elizabeth returned to her own solar, where tears of exhaustion and worry fell. She couldn't stop them and eventually, when her eyes were dry, the only thing left was a feeling of uncontrollable sorrow.

The following day, Alaric arrived home some hours after daybreak, much to Elizabeth's surprise, but it was late in the evening before he joined her in the great hall of the manor. He began to tell her of his experiences.

"We showed the rebels what the order of society is," he said. "They will not dare to raise weapons against us again in a hurry. And then I got the call to return closer to home, leaving Lord John in London. I was ordered to Burgh St Peter of all places."

With these words, Elizabeth looked up. "What is occurring there?" she asked as innocently as possible.

"You should have seen Sir Henry Despenser. What a sight. The Fighting Bishop of Norwich. He may be a man of God but he arrived with his own knights and picked up others along the way — including me. Imagine. Fighting behind such a one. You should have seen us. The local rebels thought they could outfight us." He laughed. "They were pathetic peasants with only farm labourers' weapons."

In that moment Elizabeth hated him. She had never loved him. That was saved for another, but she had never despised him. Never loathed him as she did at just then. Alaric continued unaware.

"They had billhooks and axes. Can you imagine? What they thought they could achieve, I have no idea. We cut them down like wheat to the scythe. They would not be allowed access to the abbey records on our watch."

"Surely they could not have gained access to the great abbey. The gates are fortification enough, never mind the crenelations. There is a portcullis and ditch as well."

"You are remarkably well-informed, Wife," Alaric said with a tilt of his head.

"I've visited the town in more peaceful times," Elizabeth said hastily, looking down at her skirt and brushing away imaginary crumbs.

"Yes, well, as it happens the abbey was safe but several rogues accessed the pilgrimage chapel of St Thomas. It stands near the great gates and these foolish rioters thought they could seek sanctuary there." He guffawed at the memory. "They should have thought better of that. There was no sanctuary for knaves who sought direct offence against the Church."

"People were slain inside the chapel?"

"Indeed they were, right in front of the altar. The Bishop of Norwich was in no mood to listen to such snivellers."

Elizabeth felt nauseous. She couldn't listen to another word. She might have been among those who were slain in that house of God if Master Martin had not urged them on. She would sleep in Mary's chamber this night. How could she lie with this man who had no humanity or compassion?

"I don't feel too well," Alaric said, wiping beads of sweat from his forehead. "My head is aching."

Elizabeth looked across at him. "What ails you?"

"Perhaps I have an ague coming. I stayed overnight in a tavern that really was not the cleanest. Also, I need to get this bound." He showed her his hand, where a deep wound had not healed sufficiently and showed pale yellow weeping. "Perhaps you would see to it, Elizabeth. It's not serious. A scratch merely."

"How did you come by that?" His hands looked dirty, as if he had not washed in several days.

"Some ruffian's farm implement caught me."

Elizabeth called for a bowl of warm water with vinegar and a clean cloth. When it all arrived, she bathed Aleric's hand and bound it in a cloth strip with mint and myrrh to soothe it. At least she would be spared any close wifely contact if he was unwell.

The following morning there was no sign of Alaric and so she decided to visit the families of the three men with whom she had returned from Burgh St Peter. Mistress Martin welcomed her into their small cottage, apologising for the sparsity of seating but ensuring Elizabeth had a small drink of ale and some oat biscuits.

"I'm right grateful to you, m'lady, for saving my daft 'usband as you did. It were so brave of you. I cannot imagine what got into 'im. 'Is mind was mazed by a conversation 'e 'ad with someone from a better class than 'im."

"I heard of this. I believe you mean Sir Bartholomew?"

The goodwife did not answer but the flush across her cheeks gave Elizabeth the confirmation she would have.

"I have rectified that situation. It will not happen again. Very soon I shall have a meeting with the senior sokemen and discuss the fallow land and see what might be done with it."

"That would be grand, m'lady," Mistress Martin said. "If we 'ad a bigger plot it would make such a difference to us."

It was a similar story with the wives of the other two men, after which Elizabeth went to see the wife of Master Boucher, who had not returned and must be presumed dead.

"I'm so sorry for the trouble, m'lady," she said. "I don't know what I'll do now without a man to keep me. I won't have to leave, will I?" She looked around the meagre accommodation.

"Of course not. Perhaps there will be some laundry you can do up at the manor, or maybe something in the kitchens. We'll sort something for you, until you have means of your own."

On her return to the house, Elizabeth sought a squire who had arrived with her husband, an older man, and enquired after Alaric's health.

"He's not well. I'm keeping a distance but I've seen these things before in a man after battle. I don't think it's an ague or anything for other people to fear, my lady."

"What is he showing?"

"He drools like a baby but grins at his discomfort, as if his jaw is stiff. He moans and clutches his belly as if he has spasms of pain."

"Has he eaten or drunk anything?"

"No, my lady. He cannot swallow."

"He must have ale. Perhaps soak a cloth and place it in his mouth."

"I can try, but as I say, I have seen this condition before and fear no good will come of it."

"What do you mean? Will my lord recover?" Elizabeth experienced a tremor of anxiety.

"Of that I cannot be certain, my lady. This stiffness of his jaw, you see, and the pains…" He trailed off. "Maybe it was the sin of killing people unarmed. I don't know, Lady, but maybe…" he lowered his voice, "maybe it displeased God when he entered the chapel and people were slain there."

"He was among those who entered the chapel of St. Thomas?" She hesitated to ask the next question, but she was compelled to know the answer. "Was … was he involved in the killing in there?"

"I don't know that. I was instructed to mind the horses outside, but there was a deal of shouting and screaming. It sounded like people entering the fires of Hell."

Elizabeth found the nearest seat and sank down heavily.

"I will go to him." Elizabeth hurried away with trembling legs.

On reaching her husband's chamber, she entered quietly to see him arch his back and with a rictus of pain clearly across his face, he clenched his fists. "I'll fetch a tisane," she whispered, but doubted he heard her. When she returned, she sat beside him and tried to dribble the liquid into the side of his mouth, but more ran down his cheek and into the cushion his squire had laid under his head.

Alaric died in the early hours of the morning the next day.

Elizabeth sat with him as his breathing became more shallow, until it finally ceased. She was sad at the loss of his life. She hadn't loved him, but he had been kind to her. Although she tried, she couldn't erase the picture from her mind of the people in the church at Burgh St Peter. She imagined them cowering in front of the altar, praying for the deliverance of sanctuary which was cruelly withdrawn and then he had laughed about it.

And what of Gabriel? Elizabeth could not believe he had deserted her, but if that were not the case then was he lying dead somewhere instead? That couldn't be. Surely she would know — she would feel it in her heart. And where was Master Pullen? Her anxiety increased with each hour that passed, until she couldn't concentrate and paced with fretful impatience.

CHAPTER 23

Gabriel's journey to Burgh St Peter had taken longer than he had intended or hoped. His horse had thrown a shoe and he'd had to walk several miles before finding a blacksmith who had the time to make a new one and fit it. As a consequence, he heard the curfew bells of the town before he was close enough to make the crossing of the river. The matter in hand, while important, was not urgent and Master Pullen would still be in the gaol the next day. Then he heard cries on the still night air as the watchmen shouted *couvrez-feux* — cover your fires. Although this didn't happen in the villages around his home, Gabriel understood this necessity in a town where buildings in close proximity would burn with speed and without respite.

He opted to bed down for the night where he was, but was puzzled at the number of men who were playing games or doing the same. Surely, while it was a town of some size, this number was unusual, but he didn't enquire of anyone and kept his own counsel. The last thing he needed was to become embroiled in a game of Hazard when the dice were bound to fall the wrong way for him, and he still had the toll to pay. Although he was hungry, he was thankful for a dry night, and was soon asleep under the stars.

The next morning, Gabriel arrived at the abbey's great gate and approached the porter. He was a man of the laity and of advancing years. His house would be nearby and the monks confident he wouldn't desert his post for something more exciting. It was his job to direct anyone seeking the abbey and, since the gaol was part of the abbey, Gabriel asked him for direction. The old man waved a wizened finger to the right, where a small oak door with an iron grille stood in a stone archway.

Gabriel knocked on the door, expecting a gaoler would come to the grille so he might show his letter from Lady Elizabeth and Sir Rogier, state his position, and receive Master Pullen into his care with all speed. But he was in for a shock.

After stating his task and waving the letter, locks clanked and the door swung open. The gaoler flicked his head to indicate Gabriel should enter. It was exceedingly dark inside, the only light coming from the grille in the door behind him, which the gaoler proceeded to lock. Gabriel shivered.

The prison smelled of stale humanity and the straw underfoot was sticky. He was certain he heard scrabbling in a corner, probably from rats. The man who had let him in was a layman rather than a monk. He was dressed in poor clothing and his beard was thin and wispy, and Gabriel could only imagine what the inmates had to eat, if this man was so scrawny.

"Here, let me see that again."

Gabriel reluctantly handed the man the letter.

The man seemed to take an age before grunting and looking at Gabriel. "How do I know of the truthfulness of this?"

"Look at the seal." A tone of impatience crept into Gabriel's voice, which he immediately regretted.

"Nobility, you say?" The man spat at his feet. "Wait here. No. On second thoughts, you can wait upstairs."

Gabriel followed the man, who still had hold of the letter. He was led down some steps and past a foul-smelling room with a wooden door and no light save what filtered through a tiny, barred opening, for there was no other window within. After passing another such, they came to a narrow flight of stone steps.

The gaoler turned. "Used to be the king's lodgings, this did, fifty years ago." His eyes looked aloft. "He most likely came and stayed here before going into the abbey to venerate the relic of St Oswald's arm." He sniffed and wiped his nose on his sleeve. "A place for debtors, robbers and sheep stealers, now." He chuckled. "'How the mighty have fallen,'" he quoted. "I read my Bible, see?"

"Why are you bringing me here? You have seen there is a man here who does not belong and I simply follow my lady's orders to retrieve him, as it says in that letter you hold."

"A place for forgers this be, too," said the man.

Gabriel was becoming concerned as they reached the top of the stairs, where the gaoler opened a door with a large iron key. He stood to one side and as Gabriel began to enter, the man shoved him hard and he stumbled forwards before the door banged closed behind him. He heard the sound of the lock being turned and retreating footsteps.

"Hey, you scoundrel! Come back!" Gabriel shouted and beat on the door.

When he turned, Master Pullen was in front of him.

"Master Smith, what are you doing here?" cried Pullen. "You cannot have done wrong by our masters. I don't believe such a thing!"

"I was tasked to come and recue you. A fine mess I've made of that. I had a letter of explanation of your wrongful arrest from Lady Elizabeth and Sir Rogier but that rogue had taken it."

"They are nervous. There is talk of a rebellion in this very town, like those elsewhere. Gaols have been broken into and prisoners released."

"Yes, and churches burned and records taken."

"There is little we can do but wait, I fear," Pullen said. "Someone will come tomorrow with some poor pottage — peas it will be, or something similar with rye bread. We can do little until then."

Gabriel looked at Pullen. He was dirty, he had a sore at the corner of his mouth and he was definitely thinner. He raged against what had happened. "This is so unjust!"

"At least this room has some light in it. A man told me last week that permission to fenestrate the building was given two hundred years ago, but next door where someone is being held for manslaughter and another for sheltering a murderer, there is no light at all. That window was blocked up. They'll likely hang for their offences."

Gabriel's mood lurched from anger to frustration. Talk turned to the rebellion and he wondered now whether all the men camping outside the city when he arrived were related to that. No one told them anything, but the gaolers were tense. They were vulnerable from the prisoners and they knew it.

The windows to the front of the building overlooked the market square, but it was difficult to see through the cracks in the wooden shutters. Then they heard it. The sound of horses hooves and drumbeats. Before long the chaos reached them and they rushed to see out. They heard the shouting, the screaming, the crack of metal on wood, the whine and thud of arrows, and the sound of running feet.

Someone inside the gaol shouted, "Let's get out of here before they come for us!"

"These are rebels — they may set us free," another shouted.

"They won't —" Gabriel's voice was lost in the din. Then they heard a noise on the steps beyond and the door opened. The gaoler who had imprisoned Gabriel stood to one side, indicating for them to flee. "Go, before I change my mind.

There'll be slaughter unless I'm much mistaken. These lords don't deserve our labours." He followed behind the prisoners.

"Let's take sanctuary in St Thomas' chapel," someone shouted.

Gabriel grabbed Pullen's arm. "No! Run!" he shouted. "And don't stop to look behind you."

Elizabeth met Avice returning from the fields and wondered, vaguely, where she had been. As a house servant she had little need to visit the workers outside.

"Good day," the maid said, her cheeks turning pink.

Elizabeth nodded and gave an automatic smile. The young woman hesitated and Elizabeth wondered if Avice was going to say more, but at this moment she really didn't want to speak to anyone. Perhaps Avice divined this for she didn't stop after all, but bobbed a curtsey and moved on.

It was later that evening when things became clear. She sat on a stool while Avice combed her long chestnut locks that hung down her back like waves of autumnal sunlight.

"My lady, you look beautiful tonight, but I see shadows beneath your eyes and you are distracted. Are you worried about Master Gabriel?"

"Yes, Avice, I am. He should have returned with Master Pullen days ago. There has been trouble in the town where he went and I fear for his safety. The safety of them both, of course," she added quickly.

"I understand, and he would not stay away and cause you such grief unless he had no choice. He..." Avice hesitated before taking a deep breath and continuing. "He worships you. His love is deep and enduring and he will take no other." She stopped combing and came around to stand next to Elizabeth. "He would marry you if he could, but he understands that would be impossible because of the difference in your station, and then you had to marry Sir Alaric, God rest his soul." She made the sign of the cross. "But that doesn't mean you cannot be together. Look at Lord John of Gaunt and Lady Swynford, and he's already married!"

Elizabeth was shocked and there was silence between them before Avice spoke again. "I have not offended, have I, Lady Elizabeth? For I speak only the truth. At one time I thought perhaps he had a fondness for me, but I know that is not how things are to be. I've seen the way he looks at you and it's unmatched."

Avice assumed the comb again, gently smoothing Elizabeth's hair.

"I have another beau, my lady. I was returning from the fields this morning having taken Master Oates some bread and ale. He's older than me, for sure, but he's one of your ladyship's senior sokemen and lives in a fine house with two rooms downstairs and an attic with a comfortable..." She trailed off and blushed.

Elizabeth laughed. "A comfortable what? Bed?"

"Oh no, my lady!" Avice said in an affronted tone. "He has told me about it though. He means to see you. He told me so himself, just today."

"And you like him?"

"Yes, my lady. I like him very much. He is kind and thoughtful. I could do much worse."

Elizabeth turned on the stool and looked up at Avice. "Indeed, you could. Do you like him enough to be married, though, to bear his children when the time comes and to look after him?"

Avice nodded. "I do." Then in a rush of awkwardness she added, "Forgive me, but think on what I said earlier. 'Twas not my intention to speak out of turn or to upset you, but I've seen the unhappiness in both you and Master Gabriel. Will that be all?"

As Elizabeth nodded, Avice bobbed a curtsey and left her with much to ponder.

Elizabeth didn't sleep well that night but tossed and turned, her dreams plagued by fearsome images involving bloodied bodies and piercing cries and she awoke at first light with a raging thirst. Having visited the kitchens where all was still silent, she took her mug outside and walked to the orchard that overlooked the moat and the fields beyond. Sitting under boughs heavy with fruit, not yet ripened, she breathed deeply of the early morning air and forced herself to calm. The first bells of daylight from the monastery rang the hour of prime and Elizabeth listened to the song of a blackbird. Slowly her spirit lifted and she sent a silent prayer to whoever might be listening. The lightening sky showed streaks of pearl grey and the sun, not yet showing above the horizon, was hailed with further smears of pink and cream among the canopy of veiling clouds.

Suddenly the sound of voices came from the track across the moat. Who would be about yet? Men going to work early? A tinker with his cart? She stood to see. Were her eyes betraying her? Was she seeing what she craved most in all the world or was this an illusion conjured from the depths of her desire?

Gabriel waved to another, who peeled off to one of the houses in the village, and he continued alone. He was on foot, with no horse in tow but onwards he came. He was weary. She could tell from his rounded shoulders and dragging feet. She hurried towards the bridge over the moat and as he saw her advance, his head lifted, his shoulders straightened and his pace quickened. Then he was running. Not fast, but the distance between them disappeared as she, too, ran towards him. They met in the middle of the bridge and without thought for convention she flung herself into his open arms, her cheek pressed against his heart. Her tears began to fall at last and all the tension of the last few days seeped away with them. When she looked up, his azure eyes were wet, too, and as he gazed down he smiled gently before rubbing a thumb across her cheek to wipe away all her sadness and despair.

He was home, as was she.

EPILOGUE

Lady Elizabeth Amundeville d'Albert-Swain never married again. Gabriel Smith remained as bailiff at the manor.

Lady Mary continued to live quietly. She once again began to enjoy her trips to market and bought ribbons to decorate a new gown, but she never went on her own.

Of Master Batholomew de Ath nothing was ever heard again.

Rogier married Isabelle and she lived as a good companion to her mother-in-law since her husband was away with the frequency of battles in France, on the Scottish borders, and with Wales.

The lives of Elizabeth and Gabriel were filled with love. They were quiet but complete. Lady Elizabeth gave birth to two children — Grace, then Peter, and by the grace of God she, and they, survived the ordeal. Grace had the same chestnut hair as her mother that fell in waves down her back, while Peter's was of a fashionable length but much darker and curly. Gabriel could not have been more proud of them both.

Grace often asked to look at the treasures in the copper box, and Elizabeth was more than happy to have the little one nestled on her knee as they looked at each item.

"Tell me about the peacock feather," the little girl would say as she snuggled closer to her mother.

Elizabeth smiled and gently chided her child. "Again, sweeting? You could almost tell the story of Clémence and Ruadhán to me, you have heard me tell of their love for each other so many times."

"Well, the wood carving of the apple, then. Tell me where it came from."

Elizabeth chuckled. "That was made by Gabriel."

"And it opens to show the seeds inside."

"Yes, it does."

"And those seeds represent how he loves us?"

"Yes, exactly, for each seed grows a new tree just as you are grown from us. Each tree will give us more apples to sustain us through our lives. Then the apples and their seeds on those trees will make more trees for the future. That's how our family grows and spreads throughout the years."

"Tell me why he carved this, again."

Elizabeth placed a kiss on the top of her daughter's sweet-scented hair. "When I thought I had lost him forever, he returned one beautiful morning and took an apple from a tree in the orchard. Then…" She recounted again the story of their love that still persisted so many years later. "Come, Grace. Let's go and find Gabriel and Peter."

As they approached, one small dark head was bent close to the dark curls peppered with grey of the man who Elizabeth loved more than anyone else, for he had given her these two amazing little people. When they looked up at her approach, they smiled the same cheeky grin and both waved in unison. As Grace drew close, Gabriel lifted her and swung her round so her hair streamed out behind like rays of the sun. She giggled joyously, and Peter laughed.

Gabriel's azure eyes sought Elizabeth's own over the heads of the two children and they smiled knowingly at each other. No words were necessary.

HISTORICAL NOTES

Grimsthorpe and Folkingham

The estate of Grimsthorpe exists and is well worth visiting. The current owner, Lady Jane Heathcote-Willoughby-Drummond, 28th Baroness Willoughby de Eresby lives between there and her other properties around the UK. For centuries the family have been Lords Chamberlains and the house is filled with priceless artefacts. Lady Jane was a lady-in waiting at Queen Elizabeth II's coronation.

At the time of *Mutiny at the Manor*, the King John's Tower and its attached quarters was a defensive outpost for Folkingham Castle, home to the illustrious, powerful, and well-connected Beaumont family. That castle is no longer in existence, although its site can be detected, while Grimsthorpe became a Tudor castle developed by the close friend of Henry VIII, Charles Brandon. Later additions were designed by Sir John Vanbrugh.

The site of Vaudey Abbey is hard to detect, although there are the bases of two pillars and many grassy mounds. The stones were used to build the Tudor castle. Trees have grown beside the small stream in Vallis Dei and it eerily quiet. My imagination runs wild with imaginings of the white-robed Cistercian monks silently roaming the site.

Population

Research suggests deaths during the Great Plague of 1348 reduced the population by anything from 30-50%. Among the clergy, who continued to give succour to the during this pandemic, it is believed that at least 60% died. A further outbreak in 1361 restricted the population growth that was needed to maintain agricultural demands.

The Peasants' Revolt of 1381, featured in this book, is partly the result of this population decline. The severe labour shortage ensured workers were in a strong position to demand wage increases or changes to their working regulations. Greater social mobility also began to play a part. In turn, there was strict government intervention with, for example, the Statute of Labourers which tried to fix wages at pre-pandemic levels, and restrict movement. The ruling classes tried to be oppressive, causing even more dissatisfaction and ensuring peasants simply moved on and became yeoman farmers on disused land. Some estimates say it took five hundred years for the population figures to recover.

Usuary
This is the practice of lending money at unreasonably high levels of interest for repayment and during the later mediaeval period the Catholic church forbade it. In fact they were against making *any* profit from money-lending on moral grounds, believing it was wrong to make money from those in greatest need. Penalties could be harsh.

Evasions developed where transactions were disguised as sales, where interest was hidden in the price of goods. There were penalty fees for late repayment, or compensation demanded for money lost if the lender said they might have made profit through investing the money lent.

The Crown and nobles often needed to borrow money. This was particularly true in the second half of the fourteenth century when war with France became extortionately expensive. John of Gaunt was adviser to his nephew King Richard III. When the wealthy Richard Lyons, a London merchant, landowner and ship owner, was impeached for charging 50% interest to the government, Gaunt, who was a life-long friend, defended him, ensuring his release and demonstrating his cynicism for the law. This further angered the working classes of society and John of Gaunt's unpopularity. Lyons was finally executed during the Peasants' Revolt.

Poll taxes

This is a tax levied against per head of population, rather than against land and property. It was used to finance the ongoing wars with France, but although innovative the first poll tax was regressive in its simplicity and led directly to the Peasants' Revolt. It a flat rate of one groat or four pence in 1377. Only people under the age of fourteen, the poorest, and beggars were exempt. In 1379, a second poll tax was introduced to replace the first. This had a sliding scale for payment with the wealthy paying more than the poorest, and the minimum age being raised to sixteen. It only raised a small part of what was required, was too complicated and led to evasion. Historical records show seventeen bands for payment. It was replaced less than two years later. The third poll tax was for any person over the age of fifteen and had a massive rise to twelve pence per head. Tax collectors were employed and there are accounts of bullying tactics which led to outright rebellion. There were two times for payment, January and June, but with money being short until the harvest was brought home, this amount was far beyond the reach of most labourers, leading to widespread evasion and anger.

Sokemen

These were a class of tenants who were entitled to own land which they could also sell, and they had greater freedom of movement that the poorest serfs. However, they were still subject to their lord's jurisdiction, though paying money rather than giving labour. There were far more sokemen in the east of England than anywhere else in the country, as a result of the Danelaw. Many sokemen were descended from the rank-and-file of Danish invading armies. Research suggests East Anglia had up to 80% of its male population with this status where in the rest of the country the numbers were negligible. The Soke of Peterborough is still referred to. It was a legal administrative area independent from the rest of the county council and could hold its own quarter sessions. It wasn't abolished until 1965.

Sumptuary Laws

These were to maintain social hierarchy and moral standing, and related to consumption of food, clothing and even furniture, so that people's class were easily identifiable. Types of fabric permissible for clothing, styles of shoes, and colours were strictly dictated. For example, kings and high nobles could wear purple, but the dress of a servant had to be brown. Upper classes could have silk, velvet and furs while workers were restricted to linen and wool. Even within the noble classes the use of ermine was defined so that rank was clearly identifiable. A duke and duchess would have four rows of the black tail tip of the animal on their capes, and earl and countess was three, while a baron and his wife was allowed two rows.

The laws were also to reduce extravagance and ensure reliance on local produce. Thus the sin of gluttony would be avoided and the populace would rely on food they produced at home. Imports were reduced. Churchmen believed excessive pride would also be diminished. These laws were strengthened in 1363 to ensure social mobility was restricted.

Measurements
This is a fascinating subject and there is much information on the internet. Much use was made of body parts or other things readily available. For example an inch was often the measured by the 'rule of thumb', using the top joint to the tip of the digit. Or it could be 'three barleycorns'. Thus, measurement was far from standardised in the UK and certainly not across Europe. A mile was based upon the Roman measurement, which was one thousand paces. This was divided into furlongs, chains, yards, feet and inches. A furlong was a 'furrow-long'. It was the distance that an ox could plough with resting. An acre was the area that could be ploughed by eight oxen in a team without resting. There were other measurements such as links, poles, roods and perches. It must have made bargaining very complex. Romans found the number base of 12 to be more efficient than 10 because it's divisible by 2,3,4 and 6 while ten only has the factors 2, and 5. Edward II, around 1324 tried to standardise a foot as twelve inches and subsequent monarchs aimed to ensure measurement was more unified.

Knights
The age for the ceremony of becoming a knight was more usually twenty-one, although, at times, this could be as early as eighteen, based upon battle experience and social standing. There is evidence of a young man receiving his 'dubbing' as early as twelve years of age. Rogier, in this story, received his early.

Joanna Ferrour

In this book Joanna Ferrour saved Henry Bolingbroke, son of John of Gaunt. It may seem unusual for the time that a woman would be a leader of men but Joanna's story is exceptional. She was a principal player who led the burning of John of Gaunt's Savoy Palace and the ransacking of the Tower of London. Most information about her comes from the Court Rolls, although there is no evidence that she was convicted. Indeed, there is evidence of a transfer of property against the name of her and her husband on 3rd February five years later. It is said that she and her husband, John, 'stayed the hand of an assailant' against the young Henry Bolingbroke who became King Henry IV. Perhaps this is why they received a pardon.

These historical notes are superficial through necessity, but if you've read this far, you might be inspired to read more elsewhere. I hope so. As I was researching, I frequently got lost down a 'rabbit hole' of information. The late mediaeval era is fascinating, especially when there are places of that time all around us still. I'm fortunate to live very close to the Grimsthorpe estates, Folkingham and the hamlet of Edenham.

A NOTE TO THE READER

Dear Reader,

Thank you so much for choosing this book. I enjoyed writing it and especially took pleasure in all of the research. I've referred to this is the historical notes which follow.

Please leave a short review or even a rating on **Amazon** or **Goodreads** if you have enjoyed reading *Mutiny at the Manor*. This, from knowledgeable people, is so important for authors' improvement and success, but also contributes to other readers' choice of book. I love to interact and answer questions from readers, so you are able to connect with me through Facebook, Bluesky, or X (Twitter) as RRCaraClayton.

Particular thanks go to the team at Sapere Books for knocking my rough manuscript into something so readable. They are very talented and I'm fortunate to be counted among their authors.

The next book in the Tapestry Tales Medieval Saga follows, so do keep a watch out.

Kind regards,

Cara Clayton

Sapere Books is an exciting new publisher of brilliant fiction and popular history.

To find out more about our latest releases and our monthly bargain books visit our website:
saperebooks.com